A Sincere Billionaire's Forever Love

Kristen Iten

Acknowledgments

I would like to say a special thank you to a couple of wonderful friends and fellow authors. Liwen H. and Jocelynn F., your support and encouragement made this book what it is today.

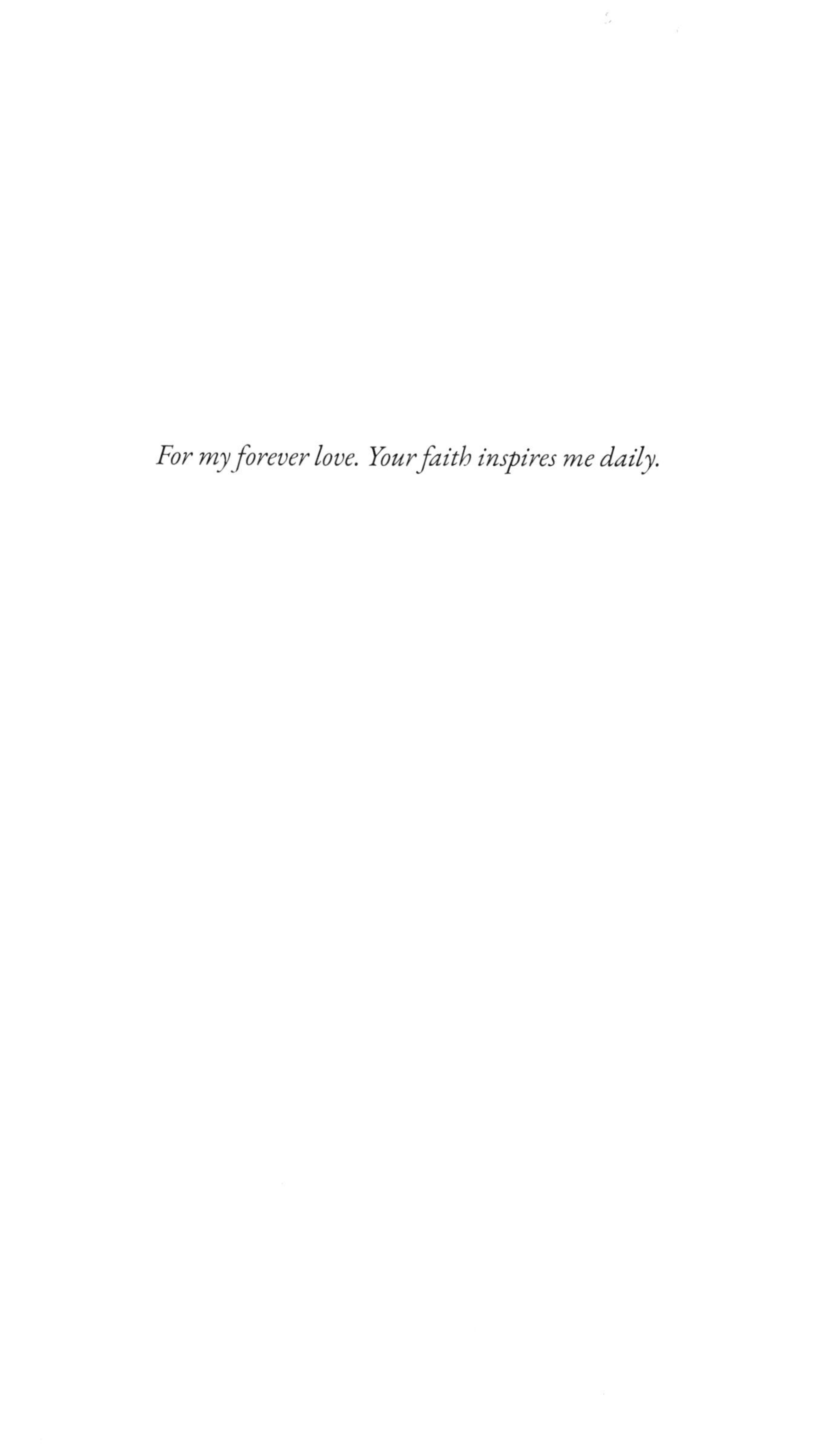

For my forever love. Your faith inspires me daily.

One

The world outside flew by in a blur as Raul De Luca gripped the steering wheel of his candy apple red race car. The number seventy-seven was painted on the nose in bold, white numerals. Double sevens for double the luck. He wasn't a particularly superstitious guy, but with his sorry driving record, he could use all the help he could get.

The speeds he reached while driving his custom-built Formula One vehicle were almost enough to free him from the grief that continually haunted the back of his mind. Almost.

But no matter how fast he went, it was always there. A part of him was convinced it always would be, and that's why he lived a fast life both on and off the race track. He had to outrun the pain. If it caught up to him—no, he couldn't let that happen. So, he raced, every year pouring more than a hundred million dollars into his hobby.

Raul's eyes narrowed, tension building in his face. The pulsating, descending tones of downshifting engines filled his ears as the racers around him slowed to navigate a sharp turn ahead. He worked the paddles on the back of his steering wheel, downshifting to keep from overshooting his angle. Exiting the turn, the red and white rumble strip sounded off as he hugged the edge of the track, searching for an opening.

The low, aerodynamic design of his car gave him an advantage when driving along the open road. But with the air turbulence coming off the race cars surrounding him, his advantage was gone. If he could just break free from the pack and find some clean air, he knew he'd leave them all behind sucking his fumes.

With every muscle in his body taut, Raul competed for the inside lane. He raced dangerously close to a sleek, black vehicle. A pair of red and gold stripes decorated the door in a diagonal pattern that stretched from one corner to the other, echoing the colors of the German flag.

A small smile spread across Raul's lips as the black car hit a section of track littered with tiny pieces of rubber shed by racers as they completed their laps. The German driver may as well have been driving on a bed of marbles for all the control he had. He spun out, ending up in the gravel trap at the side of the road.

Seeing his chance, Raul muscled his way through the opening and down the inside line. His heart raced as fast as the pistons driving his engine as he pulled away from the racers who'd had him hemmed in for so long. The leaders were still a good distance ahead, but that was okay with him. He was on pace to have his best finish ever.

The digital readout on the steering wheel told him he was traveling at two hundred seventy-two miles per hour, but he didn't need a speedometer to tell him he was tearing down the track. He reveled in the power of the g-forces as they pressed his body into the sculpted foam of his seat.

His pulse thundered in his ears as he rounded the final turn of the race and opened up the throttle, releasing every bit of horsepower his turbocharged engine had to offer.

A bolt of excitement shot through his body at the thought of the special someone waiting for him at the finish line. For the first time since calling off his engagement to another woman almost ten years ago, he'd have someone meaningful to celebrate with.

She was so different from the woman he'd almost married, never badgering him with talk of starting a family in the future. It was bad enough that his mother never let the subject rest; he didn't need it from the woman he loved, too—that's what had come between him and his fiancée, eventually damaging their relationship beyond repair.

He could never be a father; it would hurt too much. But no one seemed to understand that—not that he'd ever really tried to explain it. How were you supposed to tell someone the grief you carried around in your heart was so heavy that it actually caused physical pain at times? Maybe he should have said the words, but he didn't know how.

That's why Marie was so perfect for him. She was willing to let him be true to himself. Life was just right with only the two of them. She was all the family he would ever need.

Not even traveling at speeds in excess of two hundred miles per hour could get his heart pumping quite like the thought of the curvy Italian fireball he called his own.

Marie Maranzano sat at the final turn of the raceway with a hand lifted to her brow, shading her brown eyes from the intense light of the August sun. The wide bell sleeves of her zebra print tunic blew in the light breeze as she waited for her hunky American-born Italian racer to come into view.

She grabbed a handful of thick, dark brown hair and lifted it off her neck. Gazing off into the distance, the steely-blue silhouettes of the mountains near Sazuka, Japan beckoned her, promising cooler temperatures and relief from the relentless sun.

Raul had offered her VIP access to his stall in the paddock, but she'd opted to watch in the open air. It was the first time she'd been out of the country since college, and she didn't want to waste a single moment surrounded by the smell of oil and axle grease.

Her mind wandered as she waited for the racers to reach her end of the track again. A shiver of excitement traveled across her body as she pondered the meaning of a call she'd received in the wee hours of the morning. She'd finally gotten the green light from the Department of Human Services to become a foster mom. The thought of it both thrilled and terrified her.

Fostering was something she'd set in motion at the end of last year, before meeting Raul. She'd decided to go after her dream of becoming a mother and pursue fostering, in spite of the fact that she was still unmarried at the age of thirty-five. Her inability to land a good man was something that her mother rarely let her forget, and she was through letting it affect her chances of becoming a mother. She had so much love to give, and if she couldn't have a biological child of her own, she was determined to shower that love on precious children in need.

Now that her clearance had come through, it was only a matter of time before she stepped into the brand-new role of motherhood. She'd tried to tell Raul about her fostering plans before, but their three-month-old romance had been quite a whirlwind so far. Each time she brought up the subject, conversation seemed to swing around to something else before she could tell him.

But things were really starting to pop now. There was no time to lose—she couldn't wait to tell him. He had such a big heart; she just knew there was no way he wouldn't love the idea. Maybe—just maybe—they'd be fostering together one day. A warm shiver raced down her back at the thought of it. Dared she hope?

Staying single into her thirties hadn't been a part of her plan. The idea of marriage had consumed most of her thoughts for years, but after a certain number of failed relationships she'd figured it was time to update her relationship status to #foreveralone.

Then she met Raul. Things were different ever since he came into her life. He wasn't the typical schlep she usually dated. Where she'd once given up on the idea of ever having a lasting love, she now found herself thumbing through the bridal magazines her mother not-so-subtly left lying around her house.

Raul was special. He was a billionaire, of course, but that wasn't what was special about him. He had an appetite for life that energized her soul every time they were together. If it was his energy that drew her, it was his sincerity that kept her. He was the real deal, and that's what she loved about him.

Marie leapt to her feet as the first distant sounds of wailing engines fell on her ears.

"Come on, baby." She clapped her hands and bellowed the words before realizing that she was the only one standing. Glancing around at the wide-eyed spectators staring at her, a soft shade of pink bloomed in her olive cheeks. She sank back into her chair and nibbled the tip of a glossy red fingernail as the high pitched engines roared ever louder on their approach to the finish line.

The rolling terrain obscured the racers until they rounded the corner. The pop of their engines rattled Marie's chest. The crowd waved hundreds of tiny checkered flags as the racers buzzed by, jockeying for position. Unable to contain herself at the sight of number seventy-seven as he came into view, she jumped to her feet, throwing her fists into the air.

"That's my man—whooo!" The surge of excitement at seeing Raul speed toward the finish pushed Marie through the gallery, racing toward the finish line herself. Her voice carried over the sound of the crowd as she ran along the spectator's side of the wall lining the track, waving her arms overhead as she went. "I'm coming, baby."

Flashing her VIP badge once she reached the paddock, she was granted access to an exclusive area reserved for the racers and their teams. There he was, a mere twenty feet away on the other side of a metal gate. Her heart skipped a beat when he stood to exit his cockpit.

It was like something out of a movie. Removing his helmet, he glanced over his shoulder and flashed her a bold flirtatious smile—the same smile that had made her go weak in the knees the night they'd met in New York City.

He had swept her off her feet at a swanky charity art gala, and they hadn't touched the ground ever since. Raul seemed to have one motto in life: "What Marie wants, Marie gets." The amazing part about it was that she never even had to say what it was that she wanted. He had some sort of superpower where she was concerned; an ability to anticipate what she wanted before she even knew she wanted it. They were so in-sync it was ridiculous.

Raul tucked his helmet under his arm and scrubbed his fingers through dark, wavy hair, tousling his shaggy mane. A thousand goosebumps erupted across the surface of her skin when he hopped to the ground and made straight for her, his eyes locked onto hers. It was three months to the day since fate had brought them together, and she still got butterflies in her stomach every time she saw him.

Marie grabbed the bars of the gate in front of her and jumped up and down. "You did it!"

Raul hopped over the barricade, and stretched his arms wide. "Fifth place. How about that? Forget number seventy-seven. You're the only lucky charm I need. I should have started bringing you to all my races from the very beginning."

Fifty cameras went off when he wrapped his arms around her curvy figure and lifted her off the ground in an enormous bear hug.

"Oh, no. They're watching again," she said.

"Let them watch. I'm in love and I don't care who knows it." He flashed a million-watt smile toward an area reserved for the press, igniting another round of frantic photo snapping.

"Mr. De Luca, I am a respectable school administrator in New York City. I can't afford to be seen in cheap tabloids at the checkout line of the grocery store. We can't give them the shots they want."

There was humor in her voice, but truth in her words. She needed to protect her image if she wanted to be effective at work, and being on the wrong end of paparazzi camera lenses was not the best way to do it.

"Whatever you say, Miss Maranzano." Raul lowered her to the ground, smothering a playful grin. "I have to admit, even with as much fun as it is to be in the spotlight, hiding out from the press is pretty hot in its own kind of way."

Marie slapped his arm when he looked at her out of the corner of his eye, raising his brows several times in quick succession.

"At least tell me you're a respectable school administrator who has managed to score a week off in September to come to Italy for my next race."

"You know it. I wouldn't miss it for the world. What good is seniority if you never take advantage of it?" She threw her head back and laughed. "And it doesn't hurt that my old sorority sister is the superintendent. It helps to have friends in high places." Her next round of laughter was punctuated by a small snort that brought a smile to Raul's lips.

The sudden clatter of a crowd of children congregating at the gate leading into the paddock caught their attention. Raul wrinkled his nose and pulled his face into a grimace. "Let's hurry up and get out of here before they let those kids in."

Marie's breath froze in her chest as she took half a step backward. "What's wrong with kids?"

"There's nothing wrong with kids, as long as they're far away from me," he said with a laugh. Marie didn't feel like joining in with his laughter, and stared at him with a deadpan expression on her face.

"Come on, Marie. You know I'm only joking. Kids are fine, but I don't want to be stuck here for another hour signing autographs. I have a press conference to attend, and we've got big plans for tonight."

Kids are fine? Had he really just said that? Raul was always so over-the-top that she'd never heard him describe anything as *fine* before. Everything was always fantastic, amazing, or awesome whenever he talked. For him to say that something was just *fine* almost felt like he didn't like it at all.

She wasn't sure what he meant by the remark, and she didn't think she liked it very much. But she'd find out one way or another that night what his feelings about children really were when she told him about the call she'd received. Somehow the thought didn't bring her much comfort.

He leaned close to speak privately as they headed toward the press-free zone behind the paddock. His warm breath tickled her ear, sending a warm shiver down her spine. "I'm all yours after the press conference. There's a private island and beach with our name on it just begging for a romantic candlelight supper this evening," he said.

Once they were out of sight, Marie slipped her arm around his, deciding that she could forgive his bad joke. But was it really a joke? Sighing deeply, she resigned herself to recapture the joy she'd felt before Raul's comment about children. "Happy anniversary to us. An evening alone on the beach sounds wonderful. It'll be the perfect place to tell you my big news."

"I can't wait to hear it." He slipped his arm out of her grasp and draped it around her shoulder. "Any chance you'll give me a hint?" Raul bent down and nuzzled her with the tip of his nose. Kissing her softly on the temple, he gave her shoulders a squeeze as they walked in step toward the lot where his driver awaited them.

"Let's just say that life is about to get a whole lot more interesting," she said.

Two

Being in the limelight definitely had its perks, and Raul enjoyed each and every one of them. But being center-stage had lost a little bit of its sparkle today. He hadn't been able to slip out of the press conference as early as he'd hoped—everybody seemed to want a piece of him.

A fifth-place finish wouldn't normally be enough to warrant all the extra attention. But he was Raul De Luca, the biggest human interest story the sport of Formula One racing had seen in decades. He was the "unlucky" billionaire who, for ten years, hadn't managed to post a finish higher than eighth place; the lovable loser who seemed to have everything but a win. The media couldn't get enough of him.

The electric atmosphere of press conferences usually energized him, but today was different. It was the anniversary of the day he and Marie met. As much as he enjoyed the attention of the press, all he wanted to do was ditch them and go find a quiet place to spend time with the woman he loved.

Yes, he did love her. There was no question about that. He'd known he wanted to marry her ever since their first date. He hadn't told her, of course, but that was the finish line he was racing toward. The thought of spending the rest of his life with her caused his pulse to thunder in his ears.

Now, he stood in the hotel lobby, waiting anxiously for Marie to make her appearance. Chewing on the inside of his bottom lip, he glanced at the oversized clock on the wall behind the reception desk. She was late. A small smile tugged at the corner of his mouth as he took a deep breath. She knew what it did to him when she made him wait—it drove him wild, and they both loved it.

The soft chime of the elevator caught Raul's attention. He inhaled sharply at the sight of Marie as she stepped into the lobby, a flirty asymmetrical skirt dancing about her shapely legs with each step she took.

"I was beginning to wonder if you were going to stand me up," Raul said with a wide grin on his face.

"Stand you up? Never. I just wanted to remind you that good things come to those who wait." Marie drew her index finger along his jaw, punctuating the sentence by tapping the end of his nose.

With eyes half closed, he inhaled the spicy aroma of her perfume. It had just as much spunk and flair as Marie herself. He couldn't get enough of the scent.

"You look amazing," he said. His jaw hung open as Marie placed her hands on her delicious hips and did a mini-shimmy, the black sequin of her cowl neck shirt catching the light.

"You really think so?"

"Marie, you are the one and only woman on the planet who could pull off a sequin shirt on a date at the beach. You are…" Raul gestured toward her with open palms at a loss for words.

She placed a hand on his chest, sending a wave of heat radiating throughout his body from her touch. "Keep on talking. I think I like where this is going." A sly smile snuck onto the corner of her mouth.

Raul ran the back of his index finger down the length of her arm. He took her hand in his when he reached her fingertips, placing a soft kiss on the back of it. He gazed deeply into her brown eyes. "You are beyond description."

With lips still burning from the kiss he'd placed on her hand, images of what a future with Marie would look like flashed through his mind at lightning speed. Romance, travel, excitement—just the two of them, living life to the fullest. His heart pounded against his ribs as heated blood crept up his neck. It was a perfect future, spent with the perfect woman.

The soft thud of something hitting his leg brought him back to the present. Looking down, he saw a small ball lying on the ground next to his foot. A wide-eyed boy with sandy-brown hair stood a few paces away with his mouth hanging open.

Raul stooped over and picked up the ball. "Is this yours, buddy?"

The boy came closer. "You're one of the racers, aren't you?"

"I sure am." Raul flashed the boy a bright smile.

"Me and my dad are here for the races, but I never thought I'd meet a real racer though."

"I guess anything is possible." Raul chuckled.

A short man with thick-rimmed glasses rushed over and rested his hands on the boy's shoulders. "Mr. De Luca, I'm sorry if my son has been bothering you."

"Not at all. He was just showing us his mad skills with a ball. Are you staying here at the hotel?"

"Until the end of the week, then it's back home to Iowa for us," said the boy's father.

"Check with the reception desk tomorrow. I'll leave a little something there for your son after I get back in tonight."

The boy leapt into the air. "Really? Thanks, Mr. De Luca! Sorry I hit you."

"No harm done." Raul grinned and tossed the ball to him.

Memories of special times spent with his own father crossed Raul's mind as he watched the boy and his dad walk toward the elevator together. It had been more than ten years since his father had passed, but the loss still stung just as sharply as the day he'd heard the news. He never knew when his emotions would ambush him, bringing the pain of his father's untimely death back to the surface with a vengeance. How he missed him.

He swallowed hard against the lump forming in his throat just as Marie's pointed elbow dug into his side.

"Aww, I knew you liked kids. You were great with that little boy just now."

Why did his opinion of children matter so much to her all of a sudden? Raul didn't have time to contemplate the question before Marie stepped in close and took a fistful of his shirt in her hand. Pulling his face down to her eye level she spoke in a hoarse whisper. "Has anyone ever told you that you're one hot slice of man pie?" she asked, offering an overly exaggerated wink.

They both burst into laughter. No one could make him laugh like Marie. She had a way about her that could take any moment and infuse it with a whole new life. "No, I don't think anyone has ever told me that." He wiped tears of laughter from his eyes. "We should probably get going. The limousine is waiting."

Marie gasped. "You hired a limo to take us to the beach?"

Raul took her by the hand and led her toward a black limousine with a uniformed driver holding the door open for them. "Nothing is too good for you."

"But it's only a ten-minute drive."

Raul climbed in after her and poured an ice-cold glass of lemon-infused mineral water. "Well, we'd better get busy enjoying the ride then." He pinned her with his eyes as he handed her the drink.

Marie crossed her legs, adjusting her skirt before taking a sip. "You remembered," she said, throwing a hand to her heart.

"Of course I did. How could I forget my number-one girl's second-favorite drink? I requested it especially for you. It's not exactly the type of drink that comes standard in the wet bar of a vehicle like this."

She snorted and laughed into her glass. "I guess not, but it should be."

"Well, it will be in mine back home from now on," Raul said.

Marie glanced out the window. "Hey, isn't that the turn to get to the beach? I think the driver missed it."

Raul couldn't keep the secret any longer. "I said we were going to the beach tonight, but I didn't say which one. The beach we're heading to can only be reached by boat."

"You're going to spoil me rotten." Tingles raced up Raul's arm when Marie gave it a playful slap.

He leaned close and brushed Marie's hair back so he

could speak directly into her ear. "I haven't even begun to spoil you."

MARIE'S STOMACH DANCED WITH EXCITEMENT when their driver dropped them off at an old, lonely dock outside the city. The only boat in sight was an old fishing boat that sat low in the water.

Raul reached his hand out to Marie with the lowering evening light reflecting in his eyes. "Are you ready?" The worn boards of the dock creaked beneath his weight as he stepped out over the water.

Taking his hand, she drew her shoulders up and squealed in response as her petite legs marched in double-time to keep up with Raul's long strides. Once seated in the boat, Marie relaxed into the arm Raul wrapped around her as they set off for their island destination.

Marie ran her fingers along the weathered bench they sat on. The boat was an old craft, with scarcely a trace of its original paint left on the hull. Her imagination wandered as she considered how many trips out to sea the tiny vessel must have made over the years.

The rhythmic puttering of the antique engine propelling them almost drowned out the gentle sound of water lapping at the sides of the hull. She closed her eyes and listened to the songs of distant sea birds calling to their mates as the first hints of evening color lit up the western sky.

The smell of the day's catch filled Marie's nose as they pushed on through the calm waters of a sheltered bay en route to a secluded island, guided by an old fisherman with more wrinkles on his face than hairs on his head. The whole experience was so different from the usual luxuries Raul showered on her, but there was a richness to it that not even a fleet of limousines could match.

The wings of a hundred butterflies tickled Marie's stomach as the rocky cliffs of the island came into better view. Layer upon layer of rock rose up out of the sea and was topped with lush greenery blowing in the soft, salty breeze.

"There's only one thing on that entire island," Raul said. "It's the tiniest restaurant you've ever seen, but their seafood is epic. I've rented the whole place out for the night. No distractions tonight. Just you and me."

A shiver traveled down her spine as the hot breath from his last words caressed her neck. "You certainly pulled out all the stops for this little anniversary."

"There's no such thing as an insignificant anniversary where you're concerned." Raul gazed intently at her.

Heat rushed into her cheeks when Raul cupped them, leaning in for a kiss. With closed eyes, Marie tilted her head toward his, ready for his lips to meet hers. Before sparks could fly, the fisherman raised his voice, repeating the same word over and over again. He pointed a single, crooked finger at the water a good distance to the left.

"I think he wants us to look at something." Raul rested his forehead against hers. His lips brushed against hers as he breathed the words, causing Marie's breath to catch in her throat.

Tearing herself away from his hypnotic stare, Marie saw what all of the excitement was about. She stood suddenly, rocking the boat, giving the old man yet another reason to raise his voice.

"Dolphins!" She squealed like a schoolgirl.

With cliffs looming ahead of them, the old seaman

steered his craft toward the dock and tethered it to one of the pilings. Raul climbed out first and helped Marie onto the solid planks that led to shore.

"It's a pretty steep walk to the top, but our table is waiting on the leeward side of the island. It overlooks the channel where the dolphins usually swim this time of year. If we're lucky we'll be able to enjoy the show while we eat. I thought we could come back down here after we're done and enjoy the beach for a while before heading back for the night. It's not exactly the candlelit dinner *on* the beach that I'd originally planned, but I think this is better."

Marie squeezed his arm. "You've done it again."

"Done what?"

"You've come up with an amazing idea that I absolutely love. A sunset dinner at the top of a cliff while watching dolphins is totally me, but I never would have thought of it. It's like you know me better than I know myself. How could I have doubted you this afternoon?"

"Doubted me?"

"Yeah, that crack about the kids really shook me up at first, but after seeing you with that little boy at the hotel—and now this—it's like we were meant to be together." She interlaced her fingers with his and pulled him toward shore. "You remember how you wanted a hint about my big news?"

"Of course! Lay it on me," Raul said.

"Well, it has to do with kids. I am so beyond excited right now, but you won't get another word about it out of me until after dinner."

Raul stopped mid-stride, all the color draining from his face.

Marie placed her hand on his forehead, feeling for a temperature. "Are you feeling all right? I don't think the ride over agreed with you. Let's hurry to the top. Maybe the fresh air up there will help."

"Y-yeah, maybe."

They walked in silence, arm in arm up the stone path leading to the top of the cliffs where a romantic table for two awaited them.

Three

Raul took a linen napkin in his hand and dabbed the corner of his mouth. Dinner wasn't sitting well in his stomach. He pushed a half-eaten bowl of sashimi away, abandoning it to the center of the small round table he and Marie shared in the open air.

What was wrong with him? This was his all-time favorite Japanese dish—the reason he'd made a special trip to Japan last year. He'd become an expert at distinguishing the subtle nuances of flavor between the tuna, octopus, and squid. It was something he normally savored. But today, the rubbery texture and slimy surface of the food did nothing but turn his stomach.

But was it the food that had spoiled his appetite, or the sense of impending doom that hung over his head ever since Marie had hinted at her big news? Things were going so perfectly between them. The last thing he wanted was to spoil what they had by throwing any unnecessary complications into the mix.

Her big news had something to do with kids—that's all he could get out of her. She'd been tight lipped about the topic after she'd brought up the subject at the dock, not taking any of his bait during supper. She was dead set on keeping her secret a little longer.

Maybe he was jumping to conclusions. She did work as the principal of an elementary school in the Bronx, after all. All this fuss was probably over nothing more than news of a promotion of some sort. Fear of history repeating itself was surely clouding his mind. But there was only one way to find out for sure. This meal couldn't end fast enough, as far as he was concerned. With his constricted chest and choppy breathing, the suspense felt like it might literally kill him if he had to wait much longer.

"You don't like it?" Marie wrinkled her nose. "I can't say I blame you. I don't think that's a delicacy I could ever learn to appreciate—not my style. But throw those fish bits in with some rigatoni, slap some of Grandma Maranzano's tomato sauce on there, and bake it in the oven with a nice thick layer of mozzarella on top and I'd be all over it." Marie's laughter was as light as the breeze and eased the creases on Raul's forehead.

"I usually love the stuff. I just can't seem to get in the mood for it tonight."

"Well, I'm stuffed, and that sandy beach down there is calling my name."

"Let's get out of here, then." Raul stood and offered Marie his hand. The way the last rays of the sunlight shone in her eyes took his breath away. He could get lost in those eyes for days.

Taking a deep breath, he decided then and there that no matter what Marie's news might be, he was going to make things work with her. He'd find a way. The alternative was unthinkable. He couldn't go through life without her—not after tasting how sweet it could be with her by his side.

The walk to the beach below was much more enjoyable than the trek up the steep path. Marie took her sandals off and padded with silent steps alongside Raul. The way she hugged his arm for support on the narrow path made his heart swell. He rested a protective hand on top of hers as they descended, making sure to keep her well away from the drop off to their right.

Once they reached sea level, Raul slipped his loafers off as well. Leaving their shoes behind on a large boulder at the head of the beach, they strolled toward the gentle waves lapping at the shore.

"I can't believe we're the only two people down here," Marie said, still clinging to his arm.

"It wouldn't be very romantic if we had to share." Raul drew a heart in the sand with his bare toes. Marie stooped over to write their initials inside.

Stepping back to admire their work, she chuckled quietly. "We're just as cheesy as a couple of high-school kids in love."

"That's the way it should be." Raul took both of her hands in his and gazed into her eyes. "Let's stay this way forever, Marie. Just two kids in love. No worries. No responsibilities. I can give you that life. Just you and me—in love."

Marie tilted her head, a tender yet questioning smile on her lips. "That sounds like a wonderful dream, Raul. But we're not kids. We do have responsibilities."

"They're nothing money can't handle."

"Contrary to popular belief, there are a few things in life that money can't do. I'm about to take on some new responsibilities real soon, and I'd never try to buy my way out of them—I wouldn't want it to."

"That's my point though. You don't *have* to take on

any new responsibilities." Raul's voice pleaded against the unknown, trying to keep it at bay while enticing Marie to come to Never-Never Land with him.

Marie slipped her hands out of his and beckoned him to walk with her. "Not all responsibilities are bad. Some are wonderful. They give life meaning. Some people pray for them—I know I have."

Raul couldn't tell if it was the shifting sand beneath his feet, or the direction of their conversation, but though he struggled to move forward, he couldn't seem to get anywhere.

Marie suddenly stopped. She stepped in front of him, beaming at him with a broad smile on her face. "I can't wait another minute to tell you." She bit her bottom lip and took a deep breath. "Raul, I am going to be a mother."

The world stopped turning the moment the words left her lips, but Raul's head still spun, bringing a gut wrenching dizziness to his senses. His vision blurred as he stood speechless, eyes bouncing between Marie's stomach and her glowing eyes. "But how—we never—I don't understand..." The pounding of his heart sent a deafening rush of blood into his ears as his palms broke out into a cold sweat.

"Not like that, silly." Marie swatted playfully at Raul as laughter bubbled up from deep inside her. "I'm going to be a foster mom. I just got the call in the middle of the night last night. I've been approved. Isn't it fantastic?"

"Well, I guess it's better than having a regular kid." Raul spoke before his internal filter had a chance to come back online after the shock she'd just given him.

Marie threw her hands on her hips, raising a single brow high on her forehead. "A regular kid? What's that supposed to mean?"

"Nothing. It doesn't mean anything. I'm sorry. That came out all wrong. How is that going to work?"

"Sometime in the next few weeks I'll get a call—"

"So we still have some time?"

"What is with you? It's not a death sentence. I thought you'd be happy." Marie lowered her voice as her gaze fell to the sand at her feet. "All I've ever wanted is a family."

No! It was happening again. This was how the beginning of the end had started with his ex-fiancée. Now talk of children threatened to end the best thing that had happened to him in years. He had to get a handle on things and quick.

He and Marie were two peas in a pod. Spontaneity was the name of their game. Surely this new fascination with fostering would run its course and then things would get back to normal. All he had to do was bide his time.

It wasn't like having a child of his own—that, he could never bring himself to do. The next couple of months would be more like dating a woman who had a temporary house guest—a very short house guest. He could deal with that if it meant keeping Marie in his life.

Resting both hands on her upper arms, he looked into her eyes. "I'm sorry, Marie. You know my mouth is always getting in the way of my head. The news just really took me by surprise. If this is what you want to do, I'm happy for you."

Marie folded her arms across her chest, her lips pulled into a frown. "Maybe we should finish our walk before *my* mouth gets in the way of *my* better judgment."

Raul thought it best to hold his tongue and do as Marie suggested. There was no need to press his luck with more conversation. Suddenly the evening breeze had a chill in it that he hadn't noticed before. His eyes traveled to the inky sky above and roved over the twinkling stars looking down on them. The romance of the place made the gulf between them feel all the more empty.

This wasn't how tonight was supposed to be. Who has their first disagreement on their anniversary? Apparently, they did.

WRAPPED IN A DOWNY-SOFT HOTEL ROBE, MARIE stared at herself in the oversized mirror hanging above a luxurious solid marble vanity. Bathwater still trickled down her bare legs as her toes sank into a rug, the likes of which she'd never imagined. She wiggled them deeper into the velvety fibers, nearly causing them to disappear. Raul had booked her the presidential suite, stating that his lady deserved nothing but the best.

Raul. Usually the mere mention of his name was enough to put a giddy smile on her face, but not tonight. The memory of the look on his face at the beach earlier that evening only caused her bottom lip to tremble. His chestnut-brown eyes, rimmed with thick black lashes, had always burned with passion and playfulness toward her, but tonight they'd grown cold and sorrowful.

The jetted tub's powerful streams of water had felt like the very fingers of heaven itself, massaging her back and lower limbs as she took a late night soak. But they'd done nothing to ease the ache growing on the inside as she'd sat, turning his words over and over in her mind.

Yes, his words had been careless, but they weren't really the issue. It was the implication behind the words that still ate at her. He'd said he was happy for her—not that he was happy, or that he thought she was doing a great thing. He was happy *for her.* It felt so distant. He felt distant.

A wave of yearning washed over her without warning. She missed him. They hadn't been apart for very long, but she missed him like she'd never missed a man before. They had parted ways with a quick good-night and a peck on the cheek after getting back to the hotel. There had been no laughing. No flirting. Nothing but small, sad smiles. It was as if they'd had an earth-shattering argument without ever having said a harsh word.

What was it about the mention of children that caused such a change to come over him?

The call from the night before had sent a bolt of excitement through her when she'd heard her caseworker's words. *"It's a go. You're all cleared to foster in the state of New York."* Her heart had leapt at the realization that it was only a matter of time before she'd be selected to care for a child in crisis.

Sure it was going to be hard work, but she was up to the challenge. She was born to be a mother and nothing was going to stop her now. She'd been so sure that Raul would share in her enthusiasm that she hadn't even stopped to consider any other possibility. How could she have been so wrong?

For her, life was all about la famiglia. Growing up in a big Italian-American family had taught her that. The continuity and connection family brought to life was priceless. The past, present, and future all rolled up into one big, loud, beautiful crowd of people—all linked together by an unbreakable bond. Love. That's all she wanted. It was a tall order, but she deserved it. She deserved it just as much as the hurting children she longed to cuddle in her arms. And she was going to have it with the man she loved.

A fire ignited deep in the pit of her stomach as she leaned in close to the mirror examining her eyes, still pink from the tears she'd shed while bathing. This wasn't her. She was better than this—she was a Maranzano, for crying out loud. No one in her family had ever laid down in the face of a fight, and Raul was worth fighting for.

She stormed out of the bathroom and headed straight for the closet. Throwing on a pair of leggings and her favorite leopard print tunic, she cinched up her waist with a wide belt and prepared to do battle—not with Raul, but for him. Things had started to get serious between them and it was about time they started talking about life—real life.

Glancing up at the clock, she rolled her eyes at the late hour. Who cared what time it was? They had things to hash out—things that couldn't wait until morning. She slapped on a fresh coat of lipstick and headed straight for Raul's suite two floors down.

Four

Raul sprawled out on the bed, fingers interlocked behind his head as his eyes traced patterns on the coffered ceiling above. Deflated from the disappointing evening he'd spent with Marie, he hadn't bothered to change out of his clothes from earlier. He laid there, stone-faced, wearing a half-buttoned shirt and salt-stained pants.

Gritty sand trapped in the cuffs of his pant legs found its way onto the soft cotton sheets, but he paid it no mind. He had more important things to concern himself with—like how he was going to get back in Marie's good graces. He'd messed up tonight. An evening that started out with a bang had ended with a whimper.

The soft musical chime of a clock from the outer room of his suite heralded the passage of yet another hour. Sleep was still far from him. How could he sleep knowing that things weren't right between the two of them?

He sat up. Resting his elbows on his knees, he scrubbed his hands over his face. He had to find a way to move beyond the pain from his past before it sabotaged his present. It was quiet times like these—times when he was alone—when it hurt the most.

He'd never talked about it with Marie. Why burden the one bright ray of sunshine in his life with the grief that relentlessly clung to him? Ten long years without a reprieve. He shuddered inwardly at the merciless icy claws that promised never to release their hold on his heart. No, it was better to bury the pain deep inside, covering it over with eccentricities and outward smiles, than to confront it.

People said that the loss would get easier to bear as time went by, but they were wrong. Whenever he was still, memories of the black day he'd lost his father would surface with as much clarity as if it had happened yesterday, bringing with them the emotions he worked so hard to suppress. He could still hear his mother's broken voice as she tried to get the words out between sobs over the phone. *"He's gone."*

His father had died young—much too young—and it was all Raul's fault. Nothing had been the same since that day. How was he supposed to go on living as if nothing had happened when the single most important person in his life had been taken away?

He grabbed a handful of sheets in his hands, squeezing until his muscles trembled, knuckles turning white from the strain. What was his problem? He was a grown man. He was supposed to be strong. Each of his four brothers had bounced back and were living happy, normal lives. So why was he sitting here fighting back tears again?

Startled and then annoyed by a knock at the door, he flopped back on the bed with arms spread wide. It was probably some hotel patron who'd had a little too much *fun* on the town and had mistaken his room for their own. The knocking became insistent. He pulled himself off the bed with a deep sigh. Not in any mood to be messed with, he flung the door open with a menacing scowl on his face.

"What?" He barked the word out, but instantly softened when he saw Marie standing in front of him with a look of shock plastered on her face.

"Did I wake you? I'm sorry."

"No. I haven't slept a wink. I'm the one who should apologize." Raul's cheeks burned as he ran a hand along the back of his neck. "I figured you were some drunk beating on my door. I guess that's what I get for not using the peephole. I really am sorry."

"It seemed like a good idea to come see you a few minutes ago. Maybe I should just go. We can talk in the morning."

Raul reached out and laid a gentle hand on Marie's shoulder before she could turn to walk away. "No. Please, stay. Is everything all right?" The creases between her furrowed brow spoke volumes. She needed to talk.

Her eyes darted down the hall as if chasing the right words to say. Biting her bottom lip she gazed up into his eyes. "I feel like we said a lot tonight by not saying much of anything at all."

"I know what you mean. The way we left things—the way *I* left things has been bothering me all night. I handled everything completely wrong."

"Things won't get any better between us if we don't talk this out, you know."

"You're right. I could use a change of scenery. Let me change out of these pants and we can go down to that private nook in the lobby and talk."

"I love that idea. I'll go on down and scope out the spot. If anybody's there, I'll do something loud, obnoxious, and completely American to chase 'em away."

Raul laughed in spite of himself. No one but Marie would be able to make him laugh on a night like tonight. He needed her in his life as much as he needed air to breathe. "Sounds good to me."

Marie blew him a kiss as he watched the elevator doors close between them, sending her to the ground floor ahead of him. His pulse throbbed in his neck as near panic settled in.

It was true that they needed to talk things over, but how much did he dare share about his struggles? It was a man's duty to be a rock for the woman he loved. Who ever heard of a broken and vulnerable rock?

THE FIRE THAT HAD SURGED THROUGH MARIE'S veins as she prepared to see Raul cooled considerably when they came face to face. He had a look about him that she'd never seen before. The high cheekbones that usually supported a wide grin looked sharp and angular. Weary. He looked weary. Even when he forced a small smile, it didn't reach his eyes. Something was wrong, and she was going to get to the bottom of it.

Marie was relieved to see that the lobby was deserted this time of night. There would be no need for any shenanigans to claim a private place to hash things out.

Walking into a smaller sitting room off the main lobby, she headed for a little nook in the back corner. Stepping behind a series of traditional rice-paper screens, she found a low, square table sitting in front of a glass wall. It overlooked an immaculate rock garden, raked to perfection and illuminated by small strategically placed lanterns.

Her eyes followed the patterns of stones, carefully

placed to emulate flowing water. They didn't call it a Zen garden for nothing. After thirty seconds of gazing at it, she already felt more peaceful.

Taking a seat on one of the pillows next to the table, she rested her elbows on its glossy surface and waited for Raul to arrive. Surely he'd only be a minute or two behind her. It wouldn't take him that long to change into a new pair of pants. She needed to collect her thoughts. How did you start the kind of conversation they needed to have?

"You just spit it out, Marie." Her mumbled words sounded loud in a room that seemed to demand a reverential silence. She glanced up at the wood beams on the ceiling, their golden hues bringing warmth to an otherwise stark minimalist design.

Marie caught the familiar scent of Raul's cologne moments before his head peeked around one of the privacy screens. Strolling up to the table with a tight-lipped smile on his face, he gestured toward the pillow sitting opposite of Marie. "Is this seat taken?"

"It is now," she said with a wink. She covered the smile on her lips as she watched him struggle to figure out what to do with his long legs while lowering his body onto the square pillow in front of him.

"Criss-cross apple sauce," Marie said.

"What?"

"It's what we tell the kids at school. Fold your legs like this." She motioned to her own crossed legs.

Grabbing his knee and ankle, he forced his legs into submission, and sat awkwardly across the table from her. "So..."

"I guess we should get right to it. Let's just rip that band-aid off, shall we? What happened tonight?" Marie looked into Raul's eyes and held his gaze.

"I panicked."

"About what?"

"About us. About kids. About our future." Raul scrubbed his fingers through the silky dark waves of his hair.

"I don't understand. What's there to panic about? I said I'm going to be a foster parent. Are you worried that I won't have enough time for you anymore? 'Cause I'd never let that happen, you know. Parents make time for each other every day."

"No, it's not that," Raul said.

Marie winced inwardly as Raul bit down savagely on his lower lip while contemplating his next words.

"I never told you what broke up my relationship with my ex-fiancée, did I?"

Marie shook her head in response, her mouth suddenly dry. Her heart rate picked up speed as she sat, anticipating the revelation Raul was about to make. She'd wanted to have some real-talk, and she was about to get it.

Raul never spoke very much about this part of his past, and Marie had never given it much thought. Who would expect, or even want a man to bring up an ex-fiancée in regular conversation?

"We didn't see eye to eye when it came to kids. In the end, it led to our decision to break off our engagement."

"What was the disconnect?"

"She wanted to start a family right away and had visions of a houseful—and I mean full—of kids. I couldn't wrap my mind around that. I don't hate kids. I just couldn't see myself living that life with her. When you started talking about becoming a mother, I got scared that the same thing could happen to us."

His words melted her heart. He didn't hate children. He was scared of losing her the same way he'd lost an old love. Marie reached out for Raul's hand, a tender smile softening her features. "We don't have to let it happen to us. We can figure anything out if we're willing to put in the work."

"I'm willing, Marie. I don't want to lose what we have."

"Neither do I—my mother would never let me hear the end of it." The sound of Marie's laughter chased the heavy silence from the room.

A broad smile lit up Raul's face. "Oh, is that the *only* reason?"

Laughter that sounded painfully similar to a choking donkey continued for a few moments longer before Marie managed to quiet herself. She fanned her bright red cheeks and dabbed away the tears of joy that had pooled in her eyes. "It's not the *only* reason. But seriously, if you don't show up at my mother's for dinner on Thursday, she's going to have a conniption."

"I'll be there. I don't want to mess with Mama Maranzano."

"You don't want to mess with me either." She arched a playful brow.

Raul took both of her hands and drew tiny circles on top of them with the pads of his thumbs. "Feisty. I like it."

The fresh spark in his eyes warmed her from head to toe. They were back. Their chemistry was red hot. She knew they had a lot more to talk out once they got back to New York, but at least they were both committed to making things work. That was all she could ask for.

Five

Raul pulled up in front of a comfortable two-story home in a suburban neighborhood just outside of New York City. Hanging flower pots filled with yellow and orange marigolds swayed gently from their hooks in the ceiling of the front porch.

He couldn't help but smile at the pillows decorating the porch swing. The familiar green, white, and red stripes on each one made the long bench seat look as if it had been decorated by overweight Italian flags. It was a sight that would have made his own Italian mother's heart swell.

Silence filled his ears when he cut the engine and lingered in the leather seat of his canary yellow sports car for a few extra moments. It wasn't every day you got to have supper with your girlfriend's family for the very first time. He gripped the steering wheel with white knuckles and took a deep breath before opening the door.

The moment he stepped into the street, he heard the friendly but loud voices of the Maranzano clan, the noise traveling through the walls of Mama Maranzano's home. From the sound of it, they must have invited every living relation on the eastern seaboard to this *little* family dinner. Marie hadn't exaggerated when she'd said it was practically a national holiday whenever a Maranzano brought someone home to meet the family.

Raul dried his palms on the back pockets of his jeans before grabbing a large bouquet of flowers from the back seat, and headed up the driveway.

Selling the tech company he and his buddies had built back in their days at MIT had done a lot for his confidence —becoming a multi-billionaire straight out of college will do that for you. But somehow none of his accomplishments or his near celebrity status in the racing world seemed to matter right now. Here he was just a skinny guy with shaggy hair coming to meet the family for the first time.

His stomach churned as he neared the front door, a strange tickling sensation spreading throughout his body. The apprehension nagging at the back of his mind was only compounded by fifteen pairs of beady little eyes that seemed to follow his every move. Mama Maranzano's collection of garden gnomes scattered throughout the front lawn felt like sentinels that might spring to life at any moment to take revenge on him for daring to presume he could marry into the Maranzano family.

He grabbed the silver chain hanging around his neck, and clutched the oval pendant attached to it. Kissing it, he glanced skyward and said, "I'd appreciate any extra prayers you can spare tonight, St. Valentine." Then he tucked it into his shirt and out of sight.

A simple wooden sign hung above the door. *La famiglia* was painted on it with shaky, scrolling strokes. Somehow the sight helped to calm his nerves.

"Aunt Marie, your guy is here." A young girl with thick black hair stood on the other side of the storm door. She eyed him up and down before a herd of children ran by, sweeping her up in their excitement.

Marie appeared at the door only a moment later with a toothy grin on her face. "You're here!" She threw the clear glass door wide open and stepped onto the porch with her arms stretched out, ready to snatch him up into an enormous bear hug.

Raul took the bouquet from behind his back and held it out to her. "For you."

"Carnations? Pink carnations?" Her high-pitched, nasal exclamations let him know that he'd chosen well. "My favorite. They last so much longer than boring old roses."

"Yeah, I remembered you mentioning you weren't a huge fan of roses, but you never told me what kind of flowers you did like. I was a little nervous when I picked these out." The corner of Raul's mouth curved up into a timid smile.

Marie reached up and patted his cheek. "You're cute when you try so hard. How could any woman be disappointed when her man shows up with a bouquet of flowers for her?" Tossing her hair over her shoulder with a shake of her head, Marie struck a pose in front of Raul. "Well, what do you think?"

Taking a step back, he looked her over. Golden leggings glittered with her every move as they hugged the curves of her voluptuous thighs. She wore a sheer black button down shirt over a hot pink tank that was an eye-popping color even beneath its veil.

Marie was so unlike anyone he could ever meet while traveling in his mega-rich circles. So much of what people considered beautiful in that world was artificial. Fillers, nose jobs, body sculpting—it was all a little too much for Raul. Marie Maranzano was one hundred fifty percent natural beauty with her full lips and classic Italian profile. She was a curvy girl, and she owned it. Raul's breath hitched in his throat whenever she was near. No one had ever affected him so powerfully.

"You look spectacular. I'm hopelessly underdressed. Is that a new outfit?"

"No, silly, I'm not talking about the clothes. My hair. I curled it. What do you think?"

Raul turned her around to have a look at the thick curls cascading down her back. The fiery evening sun brought out the natural auburn highlights that normally remained hidden in lesser light. Spinning her back around to face him, he gazed into her eyes. "It's gorgeous. You're gorgeous." He pulled her into a hug and placed a kiss on the top of her head.

"Keep on talking and I'll keep on listening, lover-boy."

"Wash up." A loud voice called from inside the house.

"That's Ma. Dinner must be just about ready. We should go in." Marie tugged him toward the door, but he held his ground for a moment, excitement dancing in the pit of his stomach.

"Hold on. I've got some fantastic news I've got to tell you first—brace yourself. I just rented two neighboring villas for us in Tuscany next month during the races. They overlook miles of nothing but green, rolling hills and private vineyards. It's a spectacular view."

Marie's face didn't mirror his excitement. Instead she wore a patient, even apologetic, smile on her face. He talked even faster, as if the speed of his words could help bring her along on the visual journey he tried to paint for her. "Everything is top notch. They have arched doorways, tiled roofs, outdoor pools, and indoor pools. Honestly, it looks like the Roman baths in there, only shiny and new. It's all classic

Italian design, mixed with every touch of modern luxury you can imagine—even some you can't imagine."

"Dinner's on." The same voice called from inside. Another herd of children rushed past the door in the opposite direction. But this time there was a straggler.

A slim boy with a much lighter complexion than the other children dragged his feet as he shuffled along behind them. He had a spattering of freckles on cheeks that should have been much fuller for a boy of his tender years.

Marie reached into the house and put her arm around the boy's shoulders. Guiding him onto the porch, she stood behind him, facing him toward Raul. She ran her hands over his hair, smoothing the overgrown strawberry-blond locks out of his face.

"Raul, there's someone special I want you to meet. This is Sam. He's going to be staying with me for a bit while his mother takes care of a few legal issues. Isn't that wonderful news?"

Raul's jaw hung open for a moment before he found his voice. His heart thudded against his ribs as his mind worked double-time to process what he'd just heard. Things had moved along much faster than he'd expected. They'd gotten home from Japan less than a week ago, and already she had a foster child?

He reached an awkward hand out to the boy as if to shake hands in greeting. Sam stood still as a stone, gazing at him through guarded eyes. Raul didn't quite know what to do with his rejected hand when he withdrew it. He shoved it deep into his pocket and offered an uneasy smile.

"Let me know if my legal team can be of any assistance. I only hire the best. They've never let me down. Maybe they can help—" Raul cringed at his own words. Here he was, looking into the eyes of a child, but speaking to him like he might speak to a sixty-year-old man at the country club. He was so out of touch it wasn't even funny.

"No lawyer can help my mom. She's going to jail for good this time."

Marie wrapped the boy in a gentle embrace. "Don't say that, sweetie. Here in America everyone is innocent until proven guilty in a court of law."

The boy rolled his eyes and shrugged Marie's hug away. "I don't need a court of law to tell me mom had a room full of drugs she was selling. She ain't comin' back. That's okay though. She don't care and neither do I."

Raul's eyes met Marie's as an awkward silence filled the space between the three of them. He'd never seen Marie at a loss for words until this moment. This kid seemed sharp. He was probably right, but how did you look a child in the eye and agree with them about something so horrible?

If what the boy had said about his mother was true, she'd probably bought herself a one-way ticket on the prison train, but Raul wasn't about to say that. He couldn't very well reassure him that his mom would be back for him either.

For the first time, he realized that fostering was a very complicated undertaking—nothing like he'd thought. This child wasn't a mere house guest. He was a hurt boy, set adrift in the world by a mother who had problems of her own that were bigger than she could handle. Marie had taken on such a massive responsibility that he could feel the weight of it himself.

"There you are." A voice shockingly similar to Marie's called out from the doorway. "Are you going to keep him all to yourself, or do we get to meet the other man in your life, too?"

Raul winced inwardly at the use of the term *other man*.

He hadn't even met the family yet, and already he was playing second fiddle to the new kid on the block.

"We're coming, Teresa," Marie said, looking over her shoulder. She placed an arm around Sam's shoulders and spoke softly into his ear. "Come on in, Sammy. Life won't look quite so bleak once you've got a belly full of meatballs." She flashed Raul a sad smile as she led the boy into her mother's welcoming home.

Raul followed them into the house with a million questions swirling in his mind. The most prominent of which was about the fate of their trip to Tuscany. One of the biggest races of the season was set to take place next month, and Marie had been planning to attend for a while now.

Would the early arrival of this foster child throw a monkey wrench into their plans? A pang of guilt stabbed him in the gut at the callous selfishness of his own thoughts. Sam. The boy's name was Sam, and he was facing challenges much worse than uncertainty about a European trip.

Even so, Raul still felt a little deflated as he closed the front door behind him and headed toward a dining room teeming with Maranzanos.

Six

Marie walked into her mother's dining room, barely registering the commotion of her relatives around her. Her upbringing had made loud family get-togethers practically second nature to her. But she was keenly aware of Raul's footsteps behind her and Sam as they headed for their seats near the head of the table.

He'd handled the surprise like a champ, but guilt still pricked the back of her mind for not telling him sooner. Sam had been with her for two days. She'd wanted to tell Raul as soon as she'd heard from the boy's case worker, but hadn't been able to bring herself to make the call.

Each time she picked up the phone to tell him the news, all she could think about was how disappointed he'd be about her not being able to join him in Italy. Now she'd done it. If she'd put her big girl pants on and told him right away, he wouldn't have wasted his money booking a villa for her. She'd make it up to him... somehow.

"There you are." A short woman who looked like an older, rounder version of Marie stepped out of the kitchen holding her arms wide open. Rushing toward where they stood, she passed Marie by and wrapped Raul in a warm embrace. "It's so good to finally meet you," she said, rocking their bodies back and forth. "You're a miracle, you know that? A miracle straight out of heaven. We'd all but given up hope of Marie ever landing a man, but here you are."

"All right, Ma. You can let him go. So help me, if you strangle this one, I'm never bringing another man home to meet you." Marie got Sam settled into the chair next to hers before taking her own seat.

"Yeah, Ma. Let the poor guy go. Nobody can take the smell of your perfume for that long." A young man with jet black hair sat across the table from Raul's empty chair. He smacked his gum loudly in his teeth, an ornery glint in his dark-brown eyes.

"That's enough out of you two." Marie's mother swatted playfully in the air toward her children before catching a glimpse of the flowers Raul held. Throwing a hand over her heart, she spoke loud enough to be heard over the sound of the ten different conversations going on around them. "Oh my word! You brought me flowers?"

She took the bouquet from his hand and buried her nose in it, closing her eyes and inhaling their sweet fragrance. Turning to look over her shoulder, she said, "He's a keeper, Marie. Don't blow it with this one. He knows how to treat a lady."

Marie stifled a laugh at the confusion written on Raul's face. The bouquet wasn't for her mother, but Raul was too much of a gentleman to set the record straight. He wouldn't want to risk embarrassing her mother. His comical expression as his eyes bounced between her, her mother, and the bouquet was priceless.

"I'm Marie's mother, of course, Maria Angelina Teresa Maranzano, but you can call me Mama. Your place is right here, between me and Marie." She pulled a chair out. "You, young man, just earned yourself an extra helping of meatballs."

As quickly as she'd entered, Marie's mother exited the room with the bouquet in hand, on the hunt for a vase.

Raul sat next to Marie. He leaned close and spoke into her ear. "I'm sorry. It all happened so fast. I didn't know what to say. I'll get you a new bouquet."

"Don't worry about it. You deserve a medal for agreeing to come to this circus tonight."

"I think I like it. All the chaos really takes the pressure off. I don't have to try to impress a room of twenty-five people—just the two or three within earshot."

Marie opened a napkin, but stopped herself before tucking it into the front of Sam's shirt. She was still trying to find the right balance when it came to the child in her care. Next to her sat a little nine-year-old boy, still in need of so much nurture, but he'd practically been raising himself for who knows how long, and had grown up fast. She was determined to find the little boy inside and draw him out, but that would take time. "Here ya go, sweetie. I have a feeling you're going to need this napkin before dinner's over," she said, handing it to him with a wink.

"Yo, Raul." The same man from across the table called out. "I just gotta know. What's more temperamental, your Formula One engine or my big sister?"

"Shut it, Tony. Brothers should be seen and not heard." Marie scooped up the nearest piece of garlic bread and lobbed it at his head with a hearty laugh, spilling the basket in the process. It sailed through the air, missing Tony completely and landing on the floor behind him.

One of Marie's young nephews dove for the bread and stuffed it in his mouth just as Teresa walked into the room carrying a baby on her hip. "Get that out of your mouth. We don't eat, lick, or chew on things that have been on the floor. Get back in your seat and wait for me to get your food."

She turned to Raul. "Nice to meet you, Raul. You're a brave soul. I'm Marie's sister, Teresa." Without missing a beat, she yelled across the room to her two young boys. "We do not body-slam people in the dining room." Storming toward the youngsters, she wagged a finger in the air as she continued. "You two better get your behinds in those chairs, or so help me..."

Marie elbowed Sam, offering a warm smile. "Don't worry about those two. That's what my sister says whenever she doesn't know what to do with the twins. They'll cool it once they're stuffing their faces with dinner. Is this place too much for you?"

"I'm fine. Me and my mom lived at the shelter downtown for a long time. I'm used to rooms full of crazy people."

A single note of laughter flew out of Marie's mouth like the quack of a duck. "You're going to fit right in around here, Sammy boy."

The room quieted a few decibels when Marie's mother walked through the door toting a giant vat of spaghetti and meatballs. She frowned when she spied the spilled garlic bread on the table between Tony and Marie. "Which one of you did that?"

They pointed at each other at the same moment as if they were five years old again, trying desperately to stay out of trouble. Her mother rolled her eyes. "You better not have been throwing bread at your brother again, Marie."

Tony stuck his lip out, drawing his brows together to elicit sympathy from his mother. He held his plate out to her. "She did, Ma. So can I get the first helping? That bread nearly took my head off." He winked at Raul with an impish twinkle in his eyes.

"Stop the phony-baloney, Tony. You're a grown man. Guests get served first."

Somehow the kids at the other end of the table picked up on what their grandmother had said and started chanting, "Phony-baloney Tony".

Tony stood, stretching his five-foot eight-inch body to its full height. "What? You want a piece of this? Come and get it, you little rug rats."

"Sit down and act your age, Tony," Teresa called from the other end of the table.

Tony shrugged and took his seat. "A man's gotta defend his honor. Am I right, or am I right, Raul? You gotta back me up on this."

"Uh, yeah. Honor is an important thing to defend, especially when it's being threatened by eight-year-olds."

"Thank you!" Tony said, leaning back in his seat with a satisfied expression on his face.

Marie couldn't hold her laughter in for another moment. "Oh, Tony, will you ever grasp the concept of sarcasm?"

"Stop trying to use big school words, Marie. Nobody's impressed." A wide grin spread across Tony's face as he basked in his witty remark.

Marie reached for Raul's hand under the table and gave it a squeeze. "Are you sure you're up for this? It's not too late. You can still make a break for it. I'll hold 'em off for as long as I can."

Raul interlaced his fingers with hers and gazed into her

eyes. "I'm not going anywhere." There was something in his voice that captured her heart and released a flood of warmth that washed over her entire body. There was a promise in his eyes that couldn't be denied, but also a sadness that she couldn't help but feel she'd brought on.

Breaking herself free from his gaze, she forced a smile. "That's good, because it's too late now. You've been served." She nodded toward the mountain of noodles and meatballs her mother had just plunked down in front of him.

His eyes were as big as saucers as he surveyed his plate. "This is enough food to feed a small family."

"Or one Maranzano man," Marie said with a smirk. "I hope you're hungry. There's cannolis for dessert."

Raul shook his head slowly. "I don't think I'll be able to—"

"No one has ever successfully turned down food from my mother. Pace yourself," she said, releasing his hand and patting him on the knee.

After a solid thirty minutes of eating, Raul began to slow down. The pained look on his face said it all when her mother brought a platter filled with cannolis to the table. Marie stood and pulled Raul to his feet.

"Where do you think you're taking him?" her mother asked.

"We need to take a quick lap around the block to make room for dessert."

"I've never heard of anything so ridiculous. At least take a cannoli with you," she said, shoving the platter toward them.

"Whatever you say, Ma." She and Raul each selected a pastry overflowing with cream. "You can stick around here for a few minutes and enjoy your dessert, Sam. We won't be long." Marie leaned over and whispered into the boy's ear. "Don't be shy. Grab one for each hand."

She tousled the boy's hair and gave his shoulders a light squeeze before heading out the door with Raul. Glancing over her shoulder, the sight of the boy diving into his dessert warmed her heart. Maybe there was more of her mother in her than she realized.

Stepping out into the fresh air, Raul stretched his lean frame and rubbed his protruding belly. "I have never eaten that much in my life. I don't know where your brother puts it all."

They walked down the stairs and strolled toward the street. "That question has been plaguing the family ever since the day Tony was born." Marie smiled up at Raul and slipped her hand into his. "You did really good in there. They all love you—especially Ma."

"That's a relief. I'm used to being one of the biggest personalities in the room wherever I go, but up against that crowd? I got nothin'."

They enjoyed a light chuckle together until a stillness settled over them. They strolled down the street, hand-in-hand as the street lights flickered to life, lighting their way. A penetrating silence filled with the expectation of a difficult conversation stretched between them.

Marie finally spoke up. "You seemed a little quiet in there. Is everything okay?"

"You're not coming to Italy, are you?"

A long moment passed before Marie answered. "I'm sorry, Raul. I know how important it was to you. It was important to me too. Man, was I ever looking forward to a trip to Tuscany. It sounded like the trip of a lifetime." She hugged his arm close. "With the catch of a lifetime. I had no idea I'd get a call to take in a child so quickly."

"Why didn't you tell me? For me to find out about Sam on your mother's front porch just minutes before meeting your family—not cool. I thought we were closer than that, Marie."

Marie's dinner turned sour in her stomach. "We are. I'm sorry. I just didn't want to disappoint you about the trip and all."

"I don't suppose you could let him stay with your family for the week?"

"That poor kid has been bounced around so much in his life. What he needs the most right now is stability. It wouldn't even be legal anyways."

"I figured."

Marie heard the disappointment in his voice, and it tugged on her heart. He'd been so excited about the trip—they both had. The timing was all wrong, but she couldn't very well have turned Sam away.

"I'll pay you back for the villa," she said.

"No, you don't have to do that."

"I want to. I don't want you losing out because my plans changed without warning."

"No, really, I'll take care of it," Raul said.

"I won't take no for an answer."

He stopped short and looked down at her with a long face. "The villa goes for forty-seven thousand dollars a night."

Marie's jaw fell open. "I-I didn't realize." Her head slumped and her shoulders followed suit. "I didn't mean for this to happen. I just got the call out of the blue, you know? These kids, when the emergency strikes, there's no warning. If I hadn't taken him in, it would have meant an extended stay at a state run group home for him."

Raul wrapped his arm around her shoulders and started

walking again. "I'd be lying if I said I wasn't disappointed, but I'm not upset. This fostering gig is important to you right now—that means it's important to me, too."

Did he really just call fostering a gig? And what did he mean by *right now?* Fostering was a part of her life now. There wasn't an expiration date on it. Hadn't she made that clear back in Japan?

Feeling that she'd given him enough to deal with for one night, she decided to file the issue away for later discussion. Right now, all she wanted to do was enjoy the feeling of his strong arm around her and relax into his warmth.

After a few more minutes of walking, Marie spoke up. "What will you do about the villa? Can you get your money back?"

"No. When you're dealing with prices that high there's a pretty strict 'no-take-backsies' rule." The sound of Raul's chuckle warmed her heart. "I'll see if Jonas is free for the week."

"It still surprises me when I hear you mention the other members of the Fantastic Five by their first names like it's no big deal."

"It isn't any big deal. They're just my old college buddies. We didn't give ourselves that dumb name. That was the media's idea. If I'd had my way, I'd have thought of a way cooler name than that."

"What would you call a group of brilliant college kids who managed to become some of the youngest billionaire's in history?"

Raul scratched his chin. "I don't know, maybe something like 'The Billionaire Boys' or 'The Money Men'." That last name was so bad that they both laughed until Marie had to wipe the tears from her eyes.

"Well, I hope Jonas is free," she said.

"I'm sure he will be. He's always been there for me."

Marie dropped her gaze to the pavement beneath their feet. "Unlike me, I suppose." The somber words came out louder than she'd intended—loud enough for Raul to hear.

"That's not what I meant, Marie."

"I know. I just wish I could be there for you. It's a big race."

They found themselves stopping in front of the Maranzano family home. She'd left it feeling stuffed to the gills, but now all she felt was empty inside.

"You'd be there if you could, and knowing that is almost as good as having you there in person." He held her close for a minute before heading up the stairs leading to the porch. "Come on, let's go see how much more your mom can force-feed me."

He was putting on such a brave face, and she loved him for it. It took a real man to put someone else's needs and desires above his own. Not only was she dating a totally hot billionaire, he also had a heart of gold.

"Maybe the three of us can do something to celebrate when you get back."

Raul's eyes darted to the side. "Um... yeah. Th-that could be fun."

Was that more hesitation she saw? Raul wasn't a shy guy. What was going on? Marie sighed as they opened her mother's front door. That was one more thing to log away for a future conversation. All she had to do now was figure out when to have the talk.

Seven

Raul stood chest-deep in his Tuscan villa's luxurious indoor pool. Heated water enveloped his body, its surface as smooth as a pane of glass. He leaned back on his elbows, deep in thought as his eyes roved over the expertly fitted stones that made up the curved ceiling above his head. They'd been hewn from the ancient hills surrounding the villa, giving it an air of history and belonging.

A statue of a young Italian beauty stood on a pedestal next to the pool. Her colorless stone eyes looked on mournfully as one hand reached out toward water her life-like fingers would never touch. Raul's image reflected in the water next to hers as he stood as still as the maiden carved in stone.

He turned his back on the statue, which seemed to embody recent doubts that had taken root in his heart. Clenching his fists beneath the water's surface, he wondered if he'd ever be able to lay hold of the dreams that had felt so close when he and Marie first met.

Meeting her had opened a door to a whole new world

of hope and promise, but guilt from the past had paralyzed him years before. His inability to move beyond it threatened his prospects for a happy future a little more each day.

His mind was crowded with a conflicting jumble of thoughts, feelings, and questions. One particularly blaring question stood out from among the others. Was he cursed to live a life where the most important things—things he so desperately desired—lay just beyond his reach? He didn't know the answer, and it was tearing him up.

A wall of wide arched openings offered a magnificent view of the valley below. The rugged freedom of the low rolling hills dotted with cypress trees contrasted with the neighboring vineyards and their organized rows of grapevines.

Marie would have loved it here.

Marie. A deep, heavy breath escaped his lips. He couldn't get her out of his mind. Things would be so different if she were here. Without her, everything was colorless, tasteless—pointless. He might as well have rented a suite in the city. The opulence around him had never been intended for his enjoyment, but for hers. He understood why she couldn't come with him, but it didn't make him miss her any less.

How was he supposed to finish out the racing season without her by his side? Being a lone bachelor on the road had lost its charm the day he'd met her. It wasn't fun anymore.

He turned his head at the sound of footfalls on the hand-painted Italian tiles that decorated the floor.

"Hey man, tough loss today." A tall man with light-blue eyes walked toward the pool carrying a plush white towel. With blond locks cropped close on the sides of his head and left to grow long on top, he looked every inch a man in touch with the trends of his time.

He sat down on a lounging chair facing Raul, the platinum engagement band on his ring-finger catching the light that streamed in through the nearest archway.

Raul put on a brave front for his old college friend, relieved to have a reprieve from his own thoughts. "It's all right, Jonas. This isn't the first time I didn't place high enough in a qualifier to enter the final race. On the bright side, I guess this means I get to go home early," Raul said.

"But you were so excited to spend some time here. What was it you said? Something about exploring your roots?"

"That was before. I'm over it now."

"It's Marie, isn't it?" Jonas asked.

Raul pushed away from the pool's edge and waved his hands through the water, floating on his back. "Nothing is as simple as it was a couple of weeks ago. I don't know what's going on. How can so much feel so right between two people while so much feel so wrong? I just need to see her. When we're apart everything seems hopelessly complicated, but when we're together..."

"None of the complications matter." Jonas completed his friend's sentence with a knowing grin tugging on his lips.

"Exactly. You get it. It's probably the same way with you and Sophie, right?"

Jonas's eyes dropped to the floor at his feet, his cheeks flushing as he ran his fingers through his hair. "Sure."

"That didn't sound very convincing. What's going on, man?"

"Let's just say, I feel like the king of complications lately. I won't bore you with the details."

Raul eyed his friend. He looked tired. "You're not going to bore me."

"It's just a lot of things all coming to a head at once—business, engagement, wedding planning. It all takes a toll. Which is why I can't thank you enough for this trip. It's been great to get away for a little while."

"You should take time for yourself more often, Jonas. It sounds like you need it."

"I'm dead last on my to-do list, but I'm not here to talk about me." Jonas tossed a towel to Raul. "There's someone hanging out at my villa waiting to talk to you. She's got a business proposition that I think you'll find pretty interesting."

Raul waded through the water toward the steps. "What kind of a proposition? I'm not interested in any endorsement deals. And I'm not buying any real estate without having my lawyer look over the paperwork. I learned my lesson last year in Spain."

Jonas chuckled. "I'll let her explain the details. She's been after me for ages to get on board. I've always told her no, but I think this little project might be right up your alley. Hurry up and throw some clothes on. We've kept her waiting long enough."

RAUL WALKED INTO THE FORMAL RECEPTION room of the villa that had been intended for Marie. He'd been glad that Jonas could get some use out of the place, but it still stung a little to walk through the door knowing that Marie was on the other side of the Atlantic. His friend was only a few steps behind him when his eyes fell on a slim woman admiring the ornate fireplace against the far wall.

Her electric blue blazer stood out among the earth tones of her surroundings, making her impossible to miss.

All-business, she power-walked up to Raul with an outstretched hand. "Mr. De Luca, thank you for seeing me. I guess you know who I am?" The woman's steely-gray eyes narrowed into two thin slits as her face crunched into a smile that looked a little too forced for Raul's taste.

"No, Jonas didn't tell me a thing. What can I do for you?"

"That's not the question you should be asking. The real question is what can *I* do for you?" She dug into her pocket, produced a business card, and offered it to him. Raul took it with furrowed brows and glanced at it. Three words were printed on its white surface: Meg Monroe, Producer.

"What *can* you do for me, Meg Monroe Producer?" Raul crossed his arms firmly over his chest, preparing himself for whatever this glorified door-to-door saleswoman had in store for him.

"I can make you famous."

"I'm already pretty famous."

"In some circles, yes. But you're far from a household name."

Raul plopped down in a plush chair, dangling his leg over the arm. "And what makes you think I want to become a household name?"

Meg sat down on the couch opposite him. She crossed her legs and stretched her arms out across the back of the sofa. "You've got personality, looks, and more money than you could possibly ever need. Every man needs a mountain to take. What's left for you to conquer?"

Raul's brows knit together as his mind began to turn. He hadn't conquered much of anything in the last ten years. Life had been all about fast living, and trying to outrun the pain of his father's death. He sat up, scooting to the edge of his seat. "I'm listening."

"The way I see it, the only thing left for you to conquer is the hearts of the American public. And I want to help you do that."

"How?"

"Two words—reality television."

Raul released the breath he'd been holding and rolled his eyes. He may have enjoyed his occasional moments in the spotlight a little more than the average guy, but he did have his standards. Besides, Marie would never go for something like that. A living tabloid—that was all a reality television show was—and he knew how she felt about tabloids.

"Hear me out," she said, suddenly leaning forward and resting her elbows on her knees. "It's no secret that you thrive in the spotlight. People eat it up whenever you make the news. I could give you a platform to reach them every week. They're curious. They want to know you. People want to see how you live—to feel like they know you better than your best friend over there." She motioned toward Jonas, who hadn't spoken a word since they'd entered the room.

"And why would I want three hundred million people all up in my business? No, I don't want to be a part of any sensationalized, garbage television show."

"Neither do I." Meg's lips turned down into a severe expression as she regarded Raul through narrowed eyes. "I've followed you for quite some time now."

"Well, that's disturbing," Raul said, in a no-nonsense tone.

"Not in a stalker-ish sort of a way. I've followed you in the media. I see how your eyes sparkle when you're singled out in a press conference. You almost always give the paparazzi what they want when they track you down at your favorite haunts. Whenever you've been out of the spotlight for a while, you always manage to get yourself back in the news somehow. In short, Mr. De Luca, you like attention and there's no shame in that."

"She has a point there, Raul." The smirk on Jonas's face said it all. He was enjoying this conversation way too much.

"I think we can do without any more comments from the peanut gallery," Raul said, tossing a pillow at Jonas. "The fact remains that there are other considerations I have to make—beyond my own likes and dislikes." Marie for one. They'd never discussed reality television before, but he had a sneaking suspicion she wouldn't go for being seen living the high life on TV.

"What's holding you back?" From the looks of her stone face and commanding air, it was clear that Meg had experience getting what she wanted at the negotiating table.

"There are people in my life who need to maintain a certain level of dignity in order to perform their job. As much fun as I might have doing something like this, it just wouldn't work."

"So you *do* think it would be fun." Meg arched a single brow, the corner of her mouth curving into a nearly imperceptible smile.

"I said I *might* have fun. But it doesn't matter. I'll have to decline your offer."

"Don't be so hasty. I think you've got the wrong idea about my vision for the show. You called it 'sensationalized, garbage television' if I remember right. But that's not what this show is about. It's more of a documentary than anything else—a sort of living biography."

Raul ran a hand over his heavy five o'clock shadow,

scrutinizing every inch of the woman in front of him. She was smooth, that much was certain; a no-nonsense business woman doing everything in her power to close a deal. But if she was on the level, this whole thing just might work after all.

Of course Marie hadn't wanted to be in the public eye, but that was only because she didn't want to be featured in the tabloids. If this show was actually going to be a biographical documentary, how could she disapprove? It would practically be educational—something that the principal of a school was bound to appreciate.

"A living biography? So that means no flipping of tables or other kinds of manufactured drama."

"The only drama in the show would be the drama that you'd bring to it yourself. If you don't live a drama-filled life, there won't be any drama to put on the show. Like I said, my vision for this program is very different from your typical reality television show. We want to record you living your life. Nothing more—nothing less. We'll portray your friends in whatever light they need in order to maintain professional credibility in their daily lives."

This deal was sounding sweeter by the moment. As long as he got all of Meg's promises in writing, Marie wouldn't have anything to worry about.

Meg spoke up while Raul was still mulling over his thoughts. "I have a crew ready to start filming whenever you say the word. We can have episodes streaming on some of the biggest players in the market within a month. Everything is set up and ready to go."

"That's all it takes? One word from me?"

"Well, that and the matter of a few release forms that will need to be signed. This project has been in the works for a while now. I've just been waiting for the right man for the job, and I think I've found him in you."

The idea of starring in a television show of his own was intriguing. He was tired of life on the road, but he'd kept up the pace because of the distraction it provided him. The thought of living a normal life, spending quiet evenings at home, waking up in the same house morning after morning terrified him. He'd have too much time to think. Too much time to remember. Too much time to feel.

But if he agreed to this show, he just might be able to have his cake and eat it too. He could stay close to home, but would never have to be alone. He and Marie could have all the time together they wanted and when it was time to go home, an entourage would be awaiting his arrival. It would be next to impossible to have time to beat himself up over the death of his father if a camera were always hovering over his shoulder.

Raul stood and pulled his phone out of his back pocket. "I'll tell you what, you send the paperwork to my lawyer." He glanced at Meg's business card. "I'm texting you his number now. I'll need to have some sort of say in the final cut of the episodes. If we can work that out in a contract, I'd say you've got yourself a deal."

"Fantastic," Meg said. "I'll get our legal team to put something together and get the ball rolling. I'll see to it that your lawyer has a proposal on his desk within twenty-four hours."

Raul shook his head at the dollar signs he saw in her eyes. As soon as his text rang through on her phone she took her leave, promising to have a deal in place before he returned to the States.

The moment the door closed behind her, Raul turned

to Jonas with a wide smile on his face. "This is perfect. How did you find her?"

"I didn't. She tracked me down here. Like I said, she's been hounding me for a long time. She's wanted to do a show on one of the 'Fantastic Five' for years. What is it with that stupid name?"

"I know, right? I've always hated it," Raul said with a laugh.

"Anyways, I think she used me to get to you. You're the one with the interesting life. I'm just a boring businessman."

"Well, there's nothing boring about you, you're practically a superhero in a business suit. While the rest of us were out blowing our money like a bunch of idiots, you turned around and chose to do something amazing with your share of the profits."

A thoughtful smile spread over Jonas's face. It was the first time he'd looked completely relaxed since he'd arrived in Italy. "Saving all those jobs is a pretty great feeling." A heavy sigh escaped his lips as the smile faded from his lips. "If only they could all stay saved."

Raul's brows furrowed. "Stay saved?"

Jonas threw Raul's pillow from earlier back at him, forcing a smile onto his lips. "Never mind. This is my vacation. No shop talk allowed."

Raul chewed on the inside of his cheek, eyeing his friend. Something was going on with him, but this didn't seem like the right time to press him for details. There would always be time for that later. "I think this reality show might be just what I need, Jonas. It's something new and different that I can do close to home."

"Something that will keep you busy?" Jonas shot Raul a look that pierced through his soul. Jonas knew him all too well. "I know I introduced you to Meg, but I hope you don't let this become an obsession that keeps you from dealing with... things."

"I'm dealing with things just fine," Raul said.

"I still have that package, you know. Keeping it safe for you until you're ready to open it and see what he sent you."

A familiar tightening sensation clamped down on Raul's throat once again as tears pricked the corners of his eyes. Not now. He couldn't lose it in front of Jonas. He walked to the window and gazed out onto the open spaces to hide the emotions he wrestled with.

He hadn't thought of that package in years. If he were honest with himself, he'd have to admit that he'd pushed it out of his mind. A courier had delivered a small box the day after his father's funeral. He still remembered the icy chills that raced down his spine when he recognized his father's handwriting on the brown shipping paper covering the package. He hadn't been able to bring himself to open it.

As long as the box remained sealed, it was almost as if a part of his father were still alive. Once he finally opened it, Raul would never hear from him again. The finality of it caused his stomach to lurch. Feeling that way made no sense, but nothing about his father's death did. He had entrusted the package to Jonas later that same week.

"Thanks for holding on to it for me. I'll come pick it up soon."

"Whenever you're ready." Jonas laid a strong hand on his shoulder and squeezed. Speaking in a much lighter tone, Jonas sat in a nearby chair. "It'll be kind of exciting having a camera crew follow you around at your next race. Where is it again? Sao Paulo?"

"I'm not going to Brazil. I've decided to drop out for the rest of the season. Marie won't be able to come to any of the races. I don't want to be away from her that much—not right now. Life is... tricky at the moment. I want to stay close to home to make sure things work between us."

"Wow. I think that's the most mature thing I've ever heard you say. Props, man."

"Marie is worth it. She's always wanted to hide out from the media because she didn't want to end up in the tabloids, but a television show like this will be completely different. People will get to see the real her, not some phony story printed in a cheap paper."

"I didn't realize she had an issue with the media. Are you sure she'll be okay with this?"

"She'll love the idea." He grinned as he thought about telling her his big news. She would love it, right?

Eight

Marie sat on her back porch, soaking in the sun while sipping coffee from her favorite mug. Closing her eyes, she inhaled the cool morning air. She hoped some of the serenity of her surroundings would seep into her soul and quiet her frazzled nerves. Saturdays had always been her day to recharge, but now that Sam was in her life, she didn't know quite what to do with her time.

As the principal of an elementary school, she'd organized several dozen parties, activities, and events for the children she served. But having a child in her home was a whole new ball game. She felt lost.

Sam seemed content to stay inside watching Saturday morning cartoons, but she wanted to give him more than that. She wanted him to have opportunities to go new places and experience new things. Maybe it was the educator in her, but she wanted to broaden his horizons. More than anything else, she wanted to connect with him.

Up until now, all of her attempts had fallen flat. She'd never struck out so many times with a child before. In the months leading up to taking Sam in, she'd been certain that fostering was her calling in life, but right now she only felt like a total failure. The only thing he'd seemed to connect with since arriving at her home was the television.

The classes she'd taken to prepare for this undertaking had warned her that this could happen, but it didn't make it any easier to live through. Her heart broke each time she saw him retreat behind his tough exterior. If only she could get him to understand that he didn't have to protect himself against her.

All she wanted to do was scoop him up in her arms and hug all of his heartache away, like she'd done so many times for her young nieces and nephews after they took a tumble. But Sam's pain went much deeper than a mere skinned knee. She had to be patient and wait for him to invite her into his world.

She looked up into the clear blue sky and did her best to force the defeated thoughts out of her head. She was a Maranzano, and Maranzano women weren't quitters—especially where family was concerned. Nothing was more sacred to a Maranzano than *la famiglia*. She'd earn his trust, no matter what it took. All they needed was time, and she hoped they'd have enough of it.

Her phone buzzed on the table in front of her, jarring her from her deep thoughts. Her heart fluttered in her chest when she saw it was a text message from Raul.

Just landed. Missed you so much!

Be at your place in a half an hour.

I've got some big news.

Let's go to the beach today!

The beach! Why hadn't she thought of that? After hearing a few hints from Sam about his life before coming to live with her, she was fairly certain that he'd probably never had the chance to play on the beach. This was just another example of why Marie needed Raul in her life so badly. He always knew what to do.

She guzzled down what remained of her coffee, stuffed her phone into her back pocket, and rushed indoors to gather the things they'd need for a fun afternoon at the shore.

Taking a large wicker basket down from the top shelf of the hall closet, she headed straight for the kitchen to pack a few snacks. A smile curved her bright red lips as Grandma Maranzano's words came to mind. *"Feeding people is loving people."* It had been her motto in life.

A sense of pride rose to the surface of her heart as she thought of the generations of Maranzano women who had given so unselfishly of themselves to their families. Her eyes welled up at the realization that she was finally joining their ranks as she packed the basket for her little "family".

Raul's engine rumbled down the road as Marie topped off the basket with beach towels and sunscreen. She was ready. Excitement danced in the pit of her stomach and tumbled out of her mouth in the form of school-girl giggles. She hadn't seen him for more than a week. That was the longest they'd been apart since they had started seeing each other. She'd learned the hard way that she was no fan of long-distance relationships—no matter how brief the separation.

She called to Sam, who was still planted squarely in front of the television. "That's Raul. I'm going to go out to say hello while you finish your show. Then we're all going to go somewhere." She got no response from the boy. "Okay, well, see you in a few minutes. I'll be in the front yard if you need anything."

Marie bounded down her front steps and rushed up to

Raul with open arms. "I missed you." Raul wrapped his long arms around her as their lips met.

"I missed you too," he said.

"I have a million questions. What happened during the qualifier? How was the villa? Did Jonas like it? How—"

"Whoa, Marie." Raul laughed, raising both hands in surrender. "Slow down. There's no rush. We have the rest of our lives you know." Marie saw something smoldering in his eyes and it brought a flush of heat into her cheeks.

"Well, at least tell me what your big news is. I can't wait 'til we get to the beach. I've gotta know now."

"If we were inside, I'd tell you to sit down 'cause it's a doozy." A wild excitement flickered in his eyes, making Marie more curious than ever to hear what he had to say as she bounced on the balls of her feet.

Raul took a deep breath as he tried to contain a grin that threatened to stretch from ear to ear. "I've decided to drop out of the rest of the races this year." He threw his arms wide as if he were a grand showman who'd just performed a spectacular feat in front of a packed out theater.

Marie stood flat-footed in front of him, the smile fading from her lips. "I don't understand. Why? You love racing."

"Racing is a great distraction, but that's all it really is. Don't get me wrong, flying down the track at two hundred fifty miles per hour is pretty intense—a rush that I love, but it's not something that I can't live without." He rubbed his hands up and down Marie's upper arms, his touch releasing a warmth that spread like wildfire across her body. "You're the only thing I can't live without. I don't want to be away from you that much. Things were different when I thought you could come away with me, but with the way things are now... I'd just rather stay closer to home, you know?"

Tears blurred her vision as she rested her hand over his heart. "You'd do that for me? For us?" She whispered the words as if saying them out loud would break the spell and cause things to go back to the way they were. "I don't know what to say." A delicious lump formed in her throat from unshed tears of joy. Raul was serious about them. Serious enough to walk away from something that had been a way of life for him for the last ten years. That spoke to her—loud and clear.

"There's more," he said.

"More?"

"You're going to love it. Get this—" Raul placed one hand on each of Marie's shoulders—"I just signed a contract with a production company this morning. You're looking at the next big thing in reality television. But not just any reality TV show. It's reality television re-imagined."

Marie's brows furrowed as she tried to wrap her mind around what he'd just said. He had to be joking. "What?"

"I've got my own reality television series now. They're going to follow me around and do all of the reality TV stuff. You know, watch me eat, shop, and whatever else. Only they're going to do it in a totally classy way. Isn't that amazing?"

"Are they going to follow you *all* the time?"

"Yeah, pretty much. This is going to be perfect for us, Marie. Awesome, right?"

Marie's heart dropped into her stomach as she took a step back from Raul. "No! Not awesome at all. It's the complete opposite of awesome, Raul. I thought you said you dropped out of the races so we could be together more."

"I did. The filming schedule won't keep us apart. The

camera crew is just going to be part of the background—white noise."

"How could you do this?" The lump in Marie's throat grew, but for a different reason than before.

"Relax, Marie. You don't understand—"

"We've talked about the media before. That's why we've never gone fully public about our relationship—so I could stay out of the public eye. Now you're telling me that you're going to go out of your way to broadcast your life to the world?" The betrayal of her trust caused a hurt that was quickly turning into anger that boiled up from the pit of her stomach.

A gentle smile appeared on Raul's lips as he shook his head. "No, Marie. You don't understand. This show is nothing like a cheap tabloid. We don't have to hide from them like we did from the paparazzi. These people want to show America the real me—my life and the people I share it with. They want to tell the true story of... well, me. The whole thing is going to have a very public television vibe. It's just a biography that'll be delivered in weekly installments." He reached out and took Marie's hand. "This could be a lot of fun for us."

Marie's volume went up a couple of notches. "No, it won't. It's just going to be more time that we have to be apart because I can't be on a reality TV show no matter how much of a public TV vibe it has. I don't want the students at school to know every detail about our lives. It would be so unprofessional I can't even imagine it. And I don't think it's even legal to have Sam on a show like that. All this *big news* means is more hiding for me."

Marie slipped her hand away and put it on her hip. "You know, if this relationship is going to work, you can't go around making big sweeping decisions without talking them over with me first." Her ears throbbed with the rhythm of her pounding heart as heated blood rose into her cheeks.

Raul's eyes narrowed as he chewed the inside of his cheek. "Decisions like bringing a child into the picture? I'd call that a pretty big and sweeping decision, Marie. When did you talk to me about that again? Oh yeah, that's right—it never happened."

"That's not fair, Raul. I started that ball rolling a long time before I even met you."

"And then you dumped it on me without any warning at all."

"Dumped?" Marie's heart thundered in her ears. Her Italian blood was fuming and from the looks of it, so was Raul's.

She didn't know what made her more angry, his words, or the truth behind them. She'd known from the beginning that she handled the situation all wrong. She'd assumed too much, figuring that they'd naturally come into agreement about fostering just like they had on everything else they'd ever discussed. Time should have been set aside to talk it all through completely before she ever got the call from the department of human services, but it was too late now.

She'd messed up and it was all blowing up in her face.

Nine

Raul gazed down at Marie, a sickening concoction of acid and regret churning in his stomach. This was not the homecoming he'd imagined. He'd decided back when the two of them were in Japan that he was going to play the role of supportive boyfriend where fostering was concerned. All he'd needed to do was bide his time until Marie was ready to move on to something else. But his mouth had rebelled yet again, spewing words faster than he could contain them.

His chest expanded with a long breath as he clenched a handful of hair at the crown of his head with a white-knuckled fist. Releasing the death-grip he had on his hair, he held up his hand, and spoke in a low measured voice. "I don't want to fight with you, Marie."

He caught sight of Marie's bottom lip trembling before she bit down on it. No matter how much she tried, she couldn't seem to still her quivering chin. His shoulders sagged as her anger melted into sadness before his eyes.

"Neither do I," she said.

A long silence stretched between them. Raul massaged

his forehead with long, hard strokes that left white blotches in their wake. "I guess we could keep our relationship a secret from the camera crew." He hazarded a look into Marie's eyes and forced a tired smile. "It could be fun. A couple of thirty-somethings sneaking around like high-school kids."

He paused, seeing the uncertainty in her eyes before she lowered her gaze to the ground. He interlaced his fingers with hers and spoke in a hushed tone. "I have to do this, Marie. It's something I really need."

Marie's head snapped to attention, her eyes searching his with fresh new hurt swirling in their depths. "I thought you said I was the only thing you couldn't live without."

"Marie..." Words failed. He was frozen in place. His stomach turned sour as he felt Marie slipping further away. Part of him wanted to scream the truth. He was afraid to slow down—afraid of the pain that lived in the quiet. It had been his decision that had sent his father to an early grave, and the torment of that knowledge was relentless. He couldn't live a normal life while that ache still clung to his heart.

Marie shrugged, the corners of her mouth turning down as she stood looking utterly defeated. "I guess after years of living a glamorous life on the racing circuit, you need more excitement than an elementary school principal has to offer. I get it. I just thought we were enough for each other, you know?" Marie forced a sad smile. "I guess I was wrong. You need your show, and I need to foster."

He'd given her the wrong idea. She was all the excitement he would ever need, but she couldn't be with him at all hours of the day and night like a camera crew could. He couldn't tell her the whole truth. She'd never look at him the same way again if she knew how broken he was inside.

Hating the fact that he couldn't be straight with the woman he loved, he was unable to hold her gaze any longer. Ashamed of his own cowardice, he looked away.

Marie hugged her torso as if a gust of air had just blown down the street, replacing the August heat with an icy blast. She spoke with a voice more subdued than Raul knew was possible for his feisty Italian love. "I don't see how this can work, but I'm willing to give it a try for you."

Raul's heart broke at the sight of the tears pricking the corners of Marie's eyes. He lifted her hand to his lips and placed a soft kiss on her knuckles. "Thank you. I promise, nothing will be broadcast that you're not comfortable with. I have a contract that says so, and lawyers to enforce it. Let's forget about all of this and go enjoy the beach before it gets too late."

"Too late? It's not even ten o'clock. Do you have somewhere you need to be?"

"No, but it takes a good two and a half hours to fly to the island. If we want enough time to get there, enjoy the beach, and get the two of you home by bedtime, we'd better be going."

The word *bedtime* sounded foreign coming out of his mouth, but that was the way responsible adults talked when there were children involved—and like it or not, a child was involved.

It appeared to be Marie's turn to be at a loss for words. She stared at him with a look of trepidation in her eyes. "I figured we'd just drive to the coast. We can't go to your island."

"Why not? It's a great place for kids. I've got the private beaches, go-kart race track, and enough fun stuff to do inside to keep Sam busy for hours while you and I enjoy some much needed *us* time." He took Marie's upper arms in his hands, caressing her soft skin with the pads of his thumbs.

"Your island is out past Martha's Vineyard. That's in Massachusetts. I can't take Sam over state lines without permission from the court."

Raul clamped his mouth shut, the muscles of his jaw twitching as he considered his next words carefully. "There's an awful lot you can't do now, isn't there? This seems to be a recurring theme for us lately."

"I'm sorry. It's the law." Marie's shoulders slumped as her arms fell lifelessly at her sides.

Raul released a long breath, determined to end their time together better than they'd started it. "No problem. I'll just call my guys at the chopper and tell them that we're not going to be flying out today after all."

"You have a helicopter?" called a small voice.

Both Marie and Raul jumped at the exuberant voice of a little boy. Glancing behind Marie, he saw Sam bounding toward them with a bright expression on his face. He looked like a different child than the sullen boy he'd met at Marie's mother's home. His light-green eyes gleamed in the late-morning light.

"Yeah, a big black one." Raul ran his hand across the back of his neck, shifting his weight from one foot to the other.

"Cool. Can I have a ride in it?"

Marie draped her arm around the boy's shoulders. "I don't know, sweetie. We're still trying to decide what we're going to do today."

Sam's face fell, his high-spirits evaporating like an early morning mist at dawn. "Okay." His voice was flat and lifeless. There was the boy Raul recognized. Even though Sam had never been a part of his plan, it stung to watch the change come over him. Raul didn't want to be the one to hand the poor kid yet another disappointment in life

Raul caught Marie's eye. She seemed just as affected as he was by Sam's sudden change. "We *could* drive into the city and take a ride in my helicopter—being sure to stay in New York airspace." Raul added that last part quickly, his eyes begging Marie for forgiveness in case he'd overstepped his bounds. He desperately wanted to keep the peace between them. "If it's all right with Marie."

Sam's eyes came to life once again as he looked at her with expectation. "Can we?"

Marie hesitated a moment, her gaze shifting from Sam to Raul, and back again. "Of course we can, sweetie."

Sam dug into his pocket, produced a small black helicopter, and spun its crooked blades.

"That's a pretty cool helicopter you've got there. It kind of looks like mine," Raul said.

"I love everything that flies, but helicopters are my favorite," Sam said.

"You sound a lot like someone I used to know. He was obsessed with anything that could fly. He said when he was a boy, he dreamed of growing up to become a pilot." Raul's cheeks flushed as he remembered long conversations he'd had with his father about aviation as a child. He'd been just as eager to talk about it as Sam when he was his age.

"Did he do it?" asked the boy, with a wide grin on his face.

"No, he grew up and became a dad instead. My dad."

Sam's face fell. "Oh, I used to have a dad once. Mom said he stuck around long enough to give me a name and then ditched us."

"I'm really sorry to hear that, buddy. I don't have a dad anymore either. It stinks, doesn't it?"

Sam looked up into Raul's eyes, scrunching his freckled nose against the bright light of day. "Yeah."

Raul felt the enormous weight of that simple reply. Losing a father did stink. It had felt good to say it out loud. "Why don't we get going? The sooner we leave, the sooner we can be in the air. I'll call ahead and have lunch waiting for us on board. I bet you'll be the only kid in your class this year that will have ever eaten a cheeseburger while flying in a helicopter over New York City."

He opened the passenger door, and leaned the front seat forward to allow Sam to climb into the back.

Marie swiped a single tear off her cheek. "I'll go lock up."

Raul watched her walk back to the house as he closed the door behind Sam and rounded the front of the car. She was still at the point of tears. He reached in and turned on the ignition to get the air conditioning going for Sam. "Want to hear some tunes?"

He turned on the radio, hoping that the blasting AC and the rhythm of the music would give him some cover sound. He had to fix things with Marie before they left.

Raul hurried back to the passenger's side door and grabbed the handle as she made her way back to the curb. He was still trying to figure out what to say, when she marched right up to him and threw her arms around his neck. His hand fell away from the door and found a home on her lower back as he held her close. He had no idea what was going on, but he liked it. The old tingle was back.

Streams of tears streaked her face when she finally let go and took a step back.

"Marie, I'm sorry. I never meant to—"

Marie rested a finger on his lips to silence his apology.

"I've asked a lot of you recently—more than I had a right to. But what you did just now with Sam? It was amazing."

Raul's brows drew together as he tried to comprehend what Marie was saying to him. "So you're happy-crying, now? This is a good thing?"

Marie dried her cheeks, and nodded. "Did you see the look on his face? He hasn't smiled like that since the day he came to live with me. He's barely spoken, for crying out loud. You connected with him somehow. It was the most precious thing I've ever seen." Her chin started quivering again as fresh tears pooled in her eyes. Dabbing the tears away with the back of her hands, she sniffed loudly.

"Get it together, Marie," she said. She blew a long shaky breath through pursed lips. "Okay, I'm ready. Let's get this party started."

Raul nodded and opened the door for her. His stomach did a cartwheel when she squeezed his forearm as she stepped into the car. "You're good for him, Raul." She winked and flashed him a smile as she slid into the seat, sniffing one final time.

He closed the door for Marie and headed to the driver's side, uncertainty growing with each step he took. Peeking through the back window, he saw Sam flying his helicopter through the air, oblivious to the world around him. At that moment in time, he was nothing more than a happy child, playing with his favorite toy. The sight both warmed Raul's heart, and unnerved him.

There was a child in his back seat! He remembered well how his stomach had lurched the night Marie suggested that the three of them go out together when he got back from Italy. He'd been leery of the idea, but decided that it might not be so bad if done on his own terms. A day at the beach had seemed like the perfect idea. Surely the boy would spend most of the day on his own making sand castles—or whatever it was that kids did at the beach these days.

Now he was preparing to spend the rest of the day in close quarters with a boy he barely knew, and had planned to stay as far away from as possible. One look into Sam's wide eyes had done Raul in. It had been impossible to resist the urge to keep his hopes alive once they'd been ignited.

Sam seemed like a nice enough kid, but being around children triggered something in Raul—memories of his father and times spent with him. He had always envisioned himself walking in his father's footsteps and having kids himself one day. He used to look forward to a time when he'd share the same experiences with his own son, but that was never going to happen now. Precious moments that should have brought joy only caused his heart to ache.

He hadn't been the same since the day his father fell to his death when he crashed his ultralight aircraft. His guilt had seen to that. If he hadn't given him the money to buy the thing, his dad never would have been in the air that day. It was all his fault.

Raul was broken beyond repair, unable to enjoy any of the things he and his father used to do together. He'd decided long ago that if he couldn't be the kind of father that he'd had as a child, he wouldn't become one at all. So that was the end of that.

He knew he wasn't being rational, but grief rarely was.

Laying his hand on the door handle, Raul caught a glimpse of his reflection in the dark tinted window. His face was smiling, but his eyes weren't. So much turmoil churned inside him that he couldn't force a smile that was any more than skin deep.

Taking a deep breath, he slid his body into the supple

leather seat and gripped the steering wheel, tension building in every fiber of his body. It had been a long time since he'd been able to trust his own emotions. The last thing he wanted to do was become a teary-eyed mess in front of Marie and her charge, but there was no turning back now.

Ten

Marie sat on a stool at her kitchen island, scrolling through the pictures on her phone. A thoughtful smile rested on her lips as she relived the events of the previous Saturday. She'd spent it with Raul and Sam, and the final group selfie on her camera roll made her chuckle. Three heads were smashed together, making funny faces as they sat in a helicopter, the New York City skyline a thousand feet beneath them. The look on Sam's face was priceless.

Setting her phone down on the granite-patterned laminate countertop in front of her, she released a weary sigh. She and Raul had barely spoken during the week that had passed since their ride over the city. For a couple accustomed to talking on the phone at least three times a day when they weren't together in person, it was quite an unsettling change.

Life always got busy as the start of a new school year approached, but she knew deep down that wasn't the reason they hadn't talked much. It was just a convenient excuse. A heaviness settled over her heart at the memory of the disagreement they'd had on her front lawn.

They'd gone on to have a great day afterward, Sam especially, but things were still off. That special something that had always been so natural between them felt strained. The genuine way Raul had connected with Sam had warmed her heart. But she couldn't shake the feeling that even though things looked good on the surface, there were still deeper issues between her and Raul.

She fiddled with the wide-brimmed beach hat sitting on the stool next to her, as her eyes came to rest on the picnic basket that still sat on the counter where she'd left it the week before.

It all seemed a little silly now as it sat there mocking her. She'd romanticized that basket and what it represented way too much. Her cheeks burned as her embarrassment grew. Raul was a great guy, but they were a far cry from a family. They still had a lot to work out between them. Nothing seemed certain about their future anymore.

Sam's clumsy steps coming down the hall stairs stirred her from thought. "Do they fit?" she asked with a cheerier tone than she felt inside.

Sam stepped into the kitchen wearing a white t-shirt over a pair of neon-orange swimming trunks. "I look like a traffic cone."

"Yes, but a very visible traffic cone. This is our first trip to the beach, and I want to make sure I can spot you in the crowd." She hopped off her stool and grabbed her hat. "Come on. You can help me carry the basket to the car. It's about time to go. Raul is expecting us soon."

After loading up the sedan with everything needed for a day at the beach, she took a moment to put Raul's new address into her phone. She couldn't help but smile to herself as she typed it in.

Raul never did anything half-hearted. He'd rented a home in the swanky community of Westhampton Beach on Long Island after finding out that Marie couldn't come to his private island home with Sam in tow.

The pictures he'd texted showed pristine beaches, and a spacious home worthy of a magazine spread. Her stomach fluttered for the first time in days. If he was willing to go to all of this trouble just to be able to spend time with her, things couldn't be *that* wrong between them. They'd hit a little rough patch in the past couple of weeks, but maybe they would recover, after all. A love like theirs was worth working at.

"All buckled up?" Marie called over her shoulder. "Let's hit the road."

Marie's anticipation grew as she followed the directions the feminine voice in her phone called out. The longer they drove, the fancier their surroundings became, until it got to the point that she wondered if it was even legal for her to drive her old beater on such high-end asphalt.

"I thought we were going to the beach," Sam said.

"We are. It looks like we're almost there," she said, tapping her phone.

"Where's the ocean? All I see are giant houses."

"I'm sure we'll catch a glimpse of it soon. Try and sneak a peek between the houses. The ocean should be right over there." She motioned to the row of multi-million dollar homes on the right side of the street.

After one final bend in the road, her phone announced that they'd reached their final destination. She pulled up in front of an ultra-modern home that looked more like a work of art than a house. A series of angular glass and steel boxes were perched precariously on top of each other in a staggered pattern, creating the most unique silhouette Marie had ever seen in a home.

Her lightly rusted vehicle was reflected in the mirrored glass that stretched the entire length of the front of the house. She put the car in park on the street, knowing that her trusty old Nissan would leave a stain on the white cement driveway.

Marie stepped out of the car, shielding her eyes from the glaring sunlight beating down on her. She rounded the front of her vehicle and grunted as she pulled the over-stuffed basket from the passenger's side seat.

Plopping it on the grassy lawn, a sudden wave of fresh embarrassment washed over her. Why had she brought this basket? All it took was one look at the luxury home in front of her to tell that everything needed for a day at the beach must already be inside.

Raul came out the front door with a wide grin on his face, just as Marie considered putting the basket back in the car.

"What do you have there?" he said.

"Just a few beach necessities, but I'm sure I overpacked. You've probably got everything we need here at the house already." Marie picked up the basket, preparing to heave it back into the car. "I should probably just leave it here."

"No way." Raul reached out and took the basket from her. "Let me get that for you. This house is still only an empty shell. I mean, it's furnished, but there isn't anything homey about it yet. I just took possession yesterday. I'm sure this basket is just what we need."

He set it on the roof of the car, and stepped close to Marie with a hungry look in his eyes. Placing both hands on her upper arms, he said, "I think we skipped hello."

The husky sound of his voice caused Marie's pulse to pick up its tempo as her skin tingled beneath his touch. Oh, how she'd missed this man. The world around them faded away as his face drew ever nearer to hers. A slamming car door snapped them both out of their trance a moment before their lips touched. A freckled face stood only a foot away, staring up at them.

A stab of disappointment shot through Marie when Raul released her arms and stepped back, an awkward look on his face.

"Hi, Sam," he said. He ran a hand through his wavy hair. "Why don't we go through the house and hit the beach?"

"Okay." The boy turned and headed toward the front door with Marie and Raul following close behind. Raul leaned down and whispered in her ear. "We can save our hellos for later." He flashed a half-smile and winked before stepping into the lead to open the door for the three of them.

Marie couldn't help but gasp at her surroundings when she stepped across the threshold. The open design of the main floor offered an unobstructed view straight to the back of the house, where lightly tinted glass walls offered panoramic views of the ocean.

"This place is amazing," Marie said. Her voice sounded tiny in the massive room around them.

"It's not too bad," Raul said. "It'll do for a while until I can find a more permanent location here in New York."

"You're looking for a permanent place around here?"

"Of course. If my best girl can't come to me, I'll come to her. It's as simple as that." Raul slid his arm around Marie's waist and pulled her close, sending a shiver up her spine.

Sam let himself out the door leading to a raised deck with a spectacular view. He ran past the hot tub, leapt onto the outdoor sofa, and sat on his knees with his arms resting on the railing, looking out to sea.

"I don't think he's ever seen the ocean in person before," Marie said.

"He looks pretty into it."

Sam turned to face them the moment they stepped outside. "Can I go?" A wide grin stretched across his face.

"Let me spray you down first," Marie said.

Two minutes and a massive cloud of sunscreen later, Sam was running full force toward the ocean. "Hey, Marie," he called out as he stood in knee deep water, "can you see me?" He slapped his bright orange rear end and splashed his way deeper into the water, laughing as he went.

"I think he just made a joke," Marie said. "This place is good for him, Raul. I think *you're* good for him. I never see him light up as much as he does when you're around. Thanks for all of this."

"Anything for you, Marie." Raul rested his hand on the small of her back sending a tidal wave of goosebumps up and down her arms. "Shall we?" He gestured toward a wide set of stairs leading to the sandy beach below.

Marie put her beach hat on and walked in step down the stairs with Raul. She left her flip-flops on the bottom stair, and stepped onto the sand. Her toes curled at the shock of heat that scorched her bare skin. They strolled down the beach in the direction that Sam had wandered, Marie being sure to keep him in her sights all the while.

"I had no idea we'd have the beach to ourselves," she said.

"I sent you pictures."

"I figured those were just pictures used to sell the house.

Everyone loves the idea of a deserted beach, but I never expected to find one so close to the city." Marie stopped and worked her feet past the hot top layer of sand, wiggling her toes down into the cool grains that lay just beneath.

"Money can buy almost anything," Raul said.

"*Almost.*" Marie lifted her face to the sky and basked in the warm rays of the sun. She gazed at the white underbellies of gulls in flight over the water, allowing the rhythm of the waves lapping against the shore to steady her nerves as she gathered her thoughts. "About last week..."

"I should have never opened my big mouth. My filter doesn't work so well in the heat of the moment." Raul interlaced his fingers and rested his palms on the top of his head. He scrunched his face and took a deep breath. "I won't lie to you, Marie. I did feel pretty blindsided by your plans to foster, but I didn't handle things right. It's been bothering me all week."

"I felt the tension between us even when we weren't talking—especially when we weren't talking," Marie said, dropping her gaze.

"My stomach has been in knots. I've barely eaten since Saturday," Raul said. He looked over his shoulder toward the house and grinned. "Armand isn't exactly happy about that."

Marie giggled at the light moment they shared. "He's pretty fussy, isn't he?"

"You know French chefs. It's all about the food for them. If you don't eat Armand's food by Armand's rules, he flies off the handle. I'd fire him if his pastries weren't so good. I don't need all that drama in my life." Raul threw his head back as a rich belly laugh rolled from his lips.

Marie had missed the sound of his laughter, and couldn't bear the thought of things continuing on the way they had over the past week. "Are we going to be okay, Raul?" The words flew out of her mouth before she knew she was going to say them.

A caring expression softened Raul's features as he stepped in front of her, taking her hands in his. "Of course we will, Marie. I can't imagine life without you. We just have to play our game for a little while longer and things will all go back to normal. Promise."

"What game?"

"You know, keeping our little secret from the camera crew. If you can wait for me to finish my show, I can certainly wait for you to finish taking care of Sam."

Marie had known for a while that Raul had the wrong idea about her commitment to fostering. It was time to set the record straight.

"Raul, I think you've got the wrong idea about—"

The sudden rush of helicopter blades beating the air thundered overhead with a deafening force, cutting off Marie's words. A small low-flying chopper raced out over the water before swinging back to take another pass above them.

Shielding her eyes as best she could, Marie strained against the sand flying through the turbulent air around them. She clutched the sheer fuchsia cover-up she wore over her white tank and shorts as it blew wildly in the wind.

Hazarding a glance skyward, she caught a glimpse of a man leaning out of the open side door of the helicopter, video camera in hand. Marie's heart dropped into her stomach. The lens was trained on her and Raul while the aircraft hovered above them.

"What's going on?" Sand flew into her mouth as she battled to be heard above the sound of the helicopter.

Raul leaned close and shouted, his hair whipping across his face. "I don't know. Take Sam inside. I'll handle this."

She called out to Sam, who was already running toward the spectacle to get a better look. "Get in the house. Hurry up."

Marie struggled to get a grip on the storm of emotions brewing in her heart as she rushed toward the house, dragging Sam along behind her. Once inside, she turned to see Raul waving the pilot down. This was exactly what she knew would happen. There was no way to have a private life when a reality television show was involved. Impossible. So much for their secret relationship.

Despite the cloudless sky outside, a veil of gloom obscured her vision. She had Sam. Raul had his show. They were on a collision course with disaster and she was powerless to change any of it.

Eleven

"What do you think you're doing?" Raul tromped through shifting sand toward the helicopter that had just landed on the beach, its blades still spinning. "I told you I needed the day off. Why are you here?"

Meg Monroe pushed past the camera man, skin-tight jeans clinging to her pencil thin legs. Taking her red pumps in her hand, she hopped out of the chopper and into the sand with a dull thud. The cool look of indifference on her face fueled the fire that brewed in Raul's gut.

"I don't know what you're so upset about. I gave you the day off. All I wanted was a little aerial footage. We weren't even going to land until you signaled that you wanted us to come down. We had our shots and were about to be on our way—no interviews. No nothing."

"First of all, you don't *give* me days off—I take them. Second, when I say I'm taking a day off, that means no cameras. Period. I didn't think that was something that I'd need to spell out for you."

"To me, a day off means no work. You certainly didn't

have to break a sweat just to be filmed standing on the beach... or maybe you did." Meg folded her arms across her chest and smirked, a single brow perched high on her forehead. "It looked like things were a little hot between you and your guest. Maybe you *should* spell it out for us next time you have something you want to hide from my cameras. But keep in mind we're shooting a reality TV show. Your fans will feel cheated if you hid the juicy details of your life."

"There is so much wrong with everything you just said, I don't even know where to begin."

Meg cocked her head, oozing more of her infuriating attitude.

"Don't make assumptions about the company I keep," said Raul. "I'm not hiding anything juicy. My friend doesn't want to be on the show. It's as simple as that." It sounded strange to his ears to call Marie his friend. But he was committed to keeping their relationship a secret, if that was what it was going to take to bring Marie some peace of mind.

"The public will turn on you if they feel that you're keeping the truth from them. Fair warning," Meg said, raising both hands in surrender.

"And what truth might that be?" Raul rested both hands on his hips and pressed his lips into a thin, firm line.

"If you don't know, I'm sure I don't know either." Meg flashed a smile that looked more like a thinly veiled threat than an expression of joy. "But you will let me know if you have a change in relationship status during the course of filming, right?"

Raul's blood ran cold. He swallowed hard. Meg knew. He had to do something to throw her off the scent. He and Marie's relationship couldn't take another hit right now.

"Do you want proof that Marie and I are friends? Come on up to the house if you don't believe me."

"Oh, I believe you're friends. I just happen to think you're a whole lot more. We'll take you up on that offer. Come on, Miles." She called her last words over her shoulder to the camera man, still sitting in the door of the helicopter, polishing his camera lens.

He stepped to the ground, slinging his gear over his shoulder.

Raul held up a single finger. "No cameras."

"Leave it behind, Miles," Meg said.

"Are you kidding me? This rig is too expensive to leave sitting on the beach," Miles protested.

Meg started toward the house. "Have the pilot look after it, and come on."

Raul walked in silence with Meg toward the house, dread growing with each step he took. He'd done it now. His mouth was forever getting him into trouble. He'd invited the very people Marie wanted nothing to do with into his home. At the time, he couldn't see any other way. Meg was sharp. Maybe a little too sharp.

Stepping onto the deck, Raul heard the sound of raised voices coming from inside the house, though muffled behind the glass walls. "Why don't you two take a seat over there. I'll be back in a minute."

Meg's slight frame barely sunk into the foam cushion of the outdoor couch when she sat. "Remember what I said back in Italy?"

Raul paused with his hand on the door. "What?"

"The only drama on the show will be the drama you bring to it." She shot a pointed look over Raul's shoulder at a red-faced man in a white chef's uniform waving a ladle over his head.

Raul narrowed his eyes. "You know, you don't seem to be trying very hard to stay on my good side."

"We have a signed contract, Mr. De Luca. I'm not interested in your good side. I'm interested in your real side. I got my start in the business as an investigative journalist. My only interest is telling the whole story."

Raul jammed his free hand into his pocket to hide his clenched fist. "Just wait here while I see what's going on in there."

Meg glanced at Miles and smirked at the sound of Armand's raised voice when Raul opened the door. He turned away, knowing he had to get away from that woman before she goaded him into saying something he'd regret.

Once inside he dropped his chin to his chest and rolled his head from side to side, trying to relieve some of the tension in his shoulders. Filling his lungs with a deep breath, he took a quick survey of his surroundings.

Sam sat in the main living area, channel surfing on the sixty-inch television hanging above the fireplace, while Marie stood in the kitchen shouting to be heard over Armand's ravings.

Raul ran a hand over the length of his face and headed toward the ruckus. He walked up behind Marie and rested a hand on her shoulder. "What's going on?"

Marie and Armand answered at the same time. Raul held a hand up to Armand. "I was asking Marie."

"I walked in here and saw a pot on the stove. It was completely crusted over. I didn't see anyone around so I gave it a stir," she said.

"Gave it a stir? You destroyed it." Armand's face was a shade of red-purple that Raul had never seen on a human before.

"It looked like it hadn't been stirred for hours," Marie said.

"It hadn't! It was consommé. Consommé! You do not stir consommé. It is a travesty. Six hours of work destroyed by this... this—"

"Choose your next words carefully, Armand." Raul's stern voice and furrowed brows warned Armand to simmer down. "Marie is handy in the kitchen, and was only trying to help. I'm sure you've got plenty of other great things in the works for dinner tonight. We'll survive without consommé for one day."

Armand turned to the sink and poured the contents of the large stock pot down the drain, cramming the chunks of boiled chicken and vegetables into the disposal with the ladle he still clutched in his hand. A steady stream of French poured from his lips as he mourned the demise of his prized dish.

Raul looked at Marie. "I'm sorry about that. I'll talk to him later." He gestured for her to follow him a little way from the kitchen. "We have bigger problems to deal with than a ruined pot of chicken stock." He cast a glance toward the patio.

Marie followed his gaze. "Who are they?"

"Don't be mad. I had to invite them. Meg is my producer and Miles is one of the cameramen."

Marie's face blanched. "They're here? I thought you were going to send them away."

"I am." Raul forced an apologetic smile. "As soon as we convince them that there's nothing interesting to see here, I'll send them packing."

"What? And just how are we supposed to do that? I knew this would never work. I should just take Sam and leave."

"No, Marie, please stay. We can make this work. If you leave now, they'll be convinced we're hiding something." Raul raked his hands through is hair, taking a deep breath. "Look, it's up to you how we play this. They can't broadcast anything I don't sign off on, but I thought it was important to you that we kept our relationship a secret."

"Keeping our secret is one thing, but I'm not going to sit around lying to people. That's not who I am."

Raul caught a glimpse of Marie's glassy eyes before she turned her head away to gaze off into the distance.

"That's not who I am either, Marie. I have no intention of lying. We're going to tell them the truth minus a few key details that are none of their business." He forced a smile despite the sick feeling that had settled into the pit of his stomach. "This was the plan all along, right? We can outsmart them if we put our heads together, and I know just how to do it, too."

Every fiber of his being ached to reach out and touch Marie. He'd have paid any amount of money to be able to wrap his arms around her, reassuring her that everything would be okay. But he couldn't. Blast that glass wall—and the eyes on the other side of it watching his every move.

Standing at arm's length, the only source of comfort he had to offer was the sound of his voice. "We can do this, Marie. If we can look uninteresting enough, you won't even be on Meg's radar anymore."

A long breath puffed Marie's cheeks out as she released it, along with her frustration, into the world. "What's your plan?"

Twelve

Marie took one last reassuring look into Raul's eyes before stepping onto the deck through the door he held open for her. *Out of the frying pan and into the fire*. She pasted a phony smile on her lips and hoped the twitch at the corner of her mouth wasn't as noticeable as it felt.

She had no idea why her nerves were on such high alert. Even if Meg didn't buy their act, she couldn't do anything about it. Raul had complete veto power over the content of his reality show. Yet her stomach still churned as she walked toward a lounging chair opposite Meg. She and Raul had a plan, but somehow Marie felt like a dolphin trapped in a tuna net, desperate to break free into the open sea and put her troubles behind her.

Meg stood and smoothed her hands down the front of pants that were much too tight to hold a single wrinkle, before reaching out to shake Marie's hand. "Meg Monroe," she said with a nod that was all business. "And you must be the elusive Marie Maranzano."

"I don't know about elusive," Marie said with a slight chuckle.

Meg's lips thinned into a strained smile as she took her seat next to Miles. "What descriptor would you prefer? Secretive? Cloistered? It really must be nice to have a man like Raul so ready to cave into your demands." She cut her eyes over to Raul. "It's almost like you've got him wrapped around your little finger."

So that's how she was going to play it. Marie's smile grew cold, her eyes narrowing slightly as she prepared to face off with Meg. It was time to put her defenses up. Though Meg's barbs appeared to be laced with honey, they could still do some damage if Marie allowed them to hit their mark.

"Do I really need a descriptor?" Marie took the ice cold can of soda pop Raul offered from the chest beside the hot tub.

"It's just a habit I've developed during my time in the business," Meg said.

"I wasn't aware that television producers needed to label people," Raul said, offering Meg and Miles a beverage as well.

"I wasn't referring to that business. I also run a small online magazine. Descriptors, or labels as you call them, are the name of the game when you're writing celebrity gossip pieces."

Marie's ears burned from the surge of hot blood her racing heart pumped into them. This game of theirs just took a turn for the worse. Raul's contract didn't hold any power over what Meg could publish in her magazine. Marie took a long chug of her drink as her mind raced, searching for her next words.

Raul cleared his throat and shifted in his seat. "You

never told me that you run a gossip magazine," he said, scratching the back of his head.

"I have a feeling there's a lot we don't tell each other, Mr. De Luca." Meg turned her attention back to Marie like a hungry shark that smelled blood in the water. "Is that boy inside your son? He's cute, but doesn't look much like either of you."

"He's my foster son." Marie choked the words out, giving it her very best effort to suppress the bubble of air gathering inside from her massive intake of carbonated beverage.

"Yes, Principal Maranzano has always had a big heart," said Raul. "We met three months ago in New York City at an art gala she was coordinating. She raised a lot of money that night for her struggling school. She's inspired me to do my part for underprivileged kids as well."

Marie bit her lip. Raul had just thrown out the red herring. Hopefully it would be enough to distract Meg—it certainly caught Marie's attention. He'd gone over his plan quickly during their hushed conversation before stepping outside, but hearing him say it out loud sent a thrill of excitement racing down her spine all over again.

Meg reclined in her seat, slinging an arm over the back of the couch. "Oh, really? I never took you for a kid person. You keep very interesting company. Most wealthy men spend their time in the company of younger, beautiful women. And here you are, doing the exact opposite." Her eyes drifted to Marie and raked up and down her body. "No offense, Marie."

Marie sucked in her cheeks, pursing her lips. "None taken. Us old homely gals have to stick together."

Meg's jaw dropped only a tiny bit. "Touché." Turning

her attention back to Raul, she said, "I think I like her. She's not all sugar—there's a little bit of spice in there too."

"You can't be a pushover if you're the principle of a school in the Bronx," Raul said. "She's a tough lady, working hard to help pull her kids up and out of the cycle of poverty. That's no small feat." His eyes rested on Marie for a moment before he continued. "And I'm going to try to help her do it. We're in the planning stages of setting up a rewards program for students who meet certain academic goals."

The idea actually had Marie's heart thumping. This was something she'd wanted to do for years, but she hadn't been able to find any sponsors. She'd mentioned her dream in passing, but had never talked it out fully with Raul. This whole thing may have started as a plan to throw Meg off the scent of their relationship, but with Raul as her partner on this project, the sky was the limit. He'd demonstrated time and again that his heart was bigger than his bank account, and she couldn't wait to get to work.

"Fascinating. I had no idea you were such a philanthropist, Mr. De Luca. Here I just thought you were a billionaire playboy, with an appetite for the spotlight. You're actually a little bit human after all." Meg slapped Miles on the arm. "You learn something new every day."

Marie ground her teeth at Meg's last remark, flexing her jaw muscles wildly. "It's going to be a wonderful program. During the warm months, the kids will come down to the beach. They'll get to enjoy the good life and learn to do things they wouldn't normally be exposed to, like paddle boarding." She gestured toward a couple of boards leaning up against the deck.

"And during the cold weather, we take them out to my island where they can play on my epic go-cart track. I've got all kinds of stuff to do in the big house. Well, you've seen it," Raul said. "I filled the whole place up with more toys than I'll ever be able to play with. It's silly to let it all go to waste." He leaned back in his chair, interlacing his fingers and resting them on his stomach, apparently satisfied that their new plans were doing their job.

Marie turned at the sound of the door opening behind her. Sam stepped out into the sunlight, eyes squinted and nose wrinkled in the bright light.

"I suppose this fine young man is one of the charter members of this incentive program?" Meg said, setting her sights on Sam. "Have you come for paddle board lessons with Raul today?"

Sam's eyes grew wide as his jaw dropped with excitement. His whole demeanor came to life. "You can teach me?" His eyes were fixed on Raul.

Momentary panic flashed in Raul's eyes. "Oh, no. I'm not a teacher. I'm just the facilitator. I'm going to hire people to—" The sudden slump of Sam's shoulders seemed to cut Raul off mid-sentence. He took a deep breath, looking the boy over for a long minute. "I haven't gone out on a paddle board for a long time, but I guess I could give you a few pointers."

Sam's gloom left as suddenly as it had set in. He leapt into the air, pumping his fist and took off down the stairs, heading toward the paddle boards.

Raul stood and slipped his loose-fitting cotton t-shirt off, revealing a chiseled six-pack of abs beneath rock hard pecs. Marie couldn't tear her eyes away from the muscles she'd so often felt beneath his clothing as they embraced. It had always been obvious that he was cut, but seeing it with her eyes for the first time was a different experience entirely. Her mouth grew dry at the same moment her palms grew damp. She clutched at her stomach to still the fluttering inside.

His pecs flexed one final time as he wadded up his shirt and tossed it into his chair. “I guess I’ll say goodbye for now. I’ll see you both tomorrow.” He nodded toward Meg and Miles, then shrugged. “I guess it’s time for me to give my first lesson.”

Marie’s gaze lingered on Raul long after he’d stepped off the deck.

“He does make quite an impression, doesn’t he?” Meg said.

Marie’s face flushed. She hoped her dark sunglasses had given her enough cover to disguise the fact that she’d been staring. “I suppose he does.”

“He’s the total package. Brains, looks, and money—lots of money. Men like him always have women throwing themselves at them. Does that bother you?”

Marie’s brows drew together. “Should it?”

“You tell me.” Meg smirked, then leaned over to whisper something in Miles’s ear. She stood and offered Marie her hand once again. “If you’ll excuse me, I’ve got to go make a private call. It was a pleasure meeting you, Mary.”

Marie stretched her five foot one inch frame to its full height and removed her glasses to look Meg in the eyes. “It was a pleasure meeting you too, Peg.”

A single peel of laughter escaped Meg’s mouth. “I knew I liked you. What fun we’d have together if only you would agree to be on the show.” She sighed and shot a glance at Miles. “It’s a pity. Come on, Miles.”

Meg grabbed her candy apple red heels and power-walked off the deck while Miles stood and offered a clumsy wave goodbye.

Marie paid no attention to Meg and Miles as they

headed toward the chopper down the beach. Her eyes were fixated on one beautiful scene. Raul and Sam. She'd never seen bigger smiles on either of them. They laughed and splashed in the shallow water as if they'd known each other forever. There was something about Raul that woke Sam up and coaxed him out of his shell. She'd been right about Raul since the first moment they met—he was an extraordinary man with an amazing heart.

Visions of the same future she'd daydreamed about last Saturday slipped their way back into her mind's eye while she watched her two special guys enjoying life together. The high pitched whine of the helicopter's engine coming to life disrupted her thoughts. The dizzying blades spun faster and faster, until they lifted the aircraft off the ground.

Marie walked to the railing, slumping against it as a hundred thoughts pelted her from all sides. They'd done the best they could to put on their little charade, but Meg hadn't bought what they were selling. As much as Marie would have liked to believe that the helicopter had just borne all of her troubles away, she couldn't shake the feeling that it had only carried them off into the future.

Thirteen

The sun beat down on Raul's olive complexion, its brightness intensified by the water surrounding him. The cool ocean water lapping at his waist provided all the relief he needed from the heat of the late August afternoon. He ducked under the waves to cool his sun-kissed skin. Water sprayed in all directions when he stood, shaking his head like a wet dog.

Sam was on his hands and knees only a couple of feet away, balancing on a bright red paddle board. "Hey," he said with a giggle. "You got me wet."

Raul couldn't help but laugh at the comical face Sam put on. With furrowed brows and squinted eyes, the boy stared back at him like a grumpy little old man trying his best not to burst out into a belly laugh. Raul lifted his hand to cup his ear, the motion splashing a wall of water into Sam. "I'm sorry, what did you say? Was it something about getting wet?"

Sam yelled and threw himself off the board as if Raul's splash had overpowered him and knocked him into the sea.

Raul smiled and shook his head. The kid had personality by the bucket load.

There was something special about Sam. Raul couldn't put his finger on it, but he was drawn to the boy. Maybe it was his independence. Maybe it was the fact that he seemed to have no idea how much he actually needed people in his life. Whatever it was, spending time with him hadn't been as difficult as Raul had imagined it would be. Part of him was actually enjoying it. For the first time since Marie told him about her plans, he considered the possibility that he just might be able to survive her fostering phase after all.

Sam scrambled back onto the paddle board, and carefully got his feet underneath him.

"You sure you don't want me to steady it this time, buddy?" Raul asked.

"No, I've almost got it." Using his arms for balance, he stretched them wide, biting the tip of his tongue in concentration. The board rocked in the water as he straightened his legs, standing nearly to his full height. "I'm doing it! I'm doing—" A large wave rolled in and flipped the unsteady board, dumping Sam into the water.

Sam bobbed up and down in the water, sputtering and wiping his eyes with the paddle board floating behind him. Another large wave washed in, spinning the board and pushing it toward his head.

Without a moment to spare, Raul dug his toes deeply into the silky sand beneath his feet and lunged for the board, keeping it from smacking Sam in the back of the head. The moment he did, a searing pain shot through his left foot.

Raul threw the paddle board's tow loop over his shoulder, and wrapped an arm around Sam to guide him toward shore. "Come on, buddy. Let's take a break on the beach. It sounds like you gulped down half of the Atlantic on that one."

Still coughing, Sam nodded and waded back to shore with Raul limping along beside him. Each step sent a fresh wave of pain shooting up his leg.

Once clear of the water, Raul plopped down on the sand to examine his foot. The jagged shard of brown glass sticking out of the bottom of his foot made his stomach lurch. Blood flowed from the wound, staining the white sandy beach a deep shade of crimson.

"What happened?" Sam asked, leaning so close Raul could feel his hot breath on the wound.

"I guess you still have to watch your step even on a million dollar beach," Raul said. "I suppose I'm done in the water for today. I'd attract every shark in the ocean if I went back out there like this."

Sam laughed. "I think I'll stick to building sand castles for now, too," he said.

"What happened?" Marie's voice called out over the increasing sound of the waves.

Raul glanced over his shoulder to see Marie running toward them, her fuchsia cover-up flying out behind her.

"I just stepped on a piece of glass. No big deal."

"I'll be the judge of that. Give me your foot." Marie jerked her head away and clamped her eyes shut at the sight of the wound.

"It's a good thing you didn't decide to go into the medical field. Your bedside manner is about the worst I've ever seen." Raul winked at Sam.

"How can you call this no big deal? Did you happen to notice the giant chunk of beer bottle stuck in your foot?"

Raul's lips twitched as he tried to suppress his smile.

Marie was cute when she was flustered. "Yeah, it was kind of hard to miss."

"Well, it's not 'no big deal'. Come on. Let's get you to the deck. I need to clean that up."

"Is he going to be okay, Marie?" Sam's brows knit together, concern evident in his shaky voice.

"Oh, yes, sweetie. He's going to be just fine after I'm done with him. Do you want to keep playing here in the sand?"

"Yeah, I've always wanted to build a sand castle. I never thought I'd see a beach in real life. I don't want to waste my only chance."

Marie cleared her throat and turned her head away. "Seize the day, sweetheart."

Raul saw the hint of tears forming in the corners of Marie's eyes before she took his arm and slid it over her head and around her shoulders.

"Lean on me," she said.

Once they were out of Sam's earshot he gave her shoulders a squeeze. "What were the tears for back there?"

Marie sniffed. "It's just that sweet boy. It breaks my heart to think of the life he's lived up to now—the life he'll have to go back to some day. Did you hear him? He never thought he'd see the beach with his own eyes. I don't think he expects to see it again either, from the sound of it. Something as simple as a day at the beach, and he considers it a once-in-a-lifetime experience."

"I see what you mean." Now that Marie pointed it out, it tugged on his heart strings, too. A kid like Sam deserved more out of life. Much more.

Raul winced when he tried to put weight on his injured foot to climb the stairs.

"This isn't going to work. You sit here while I go and get what I need to patch you up," Marie said.

"No, it's fine. I can make it to the—"

"Nonsense! There's no need to put on a tough guy act for me. It's plain to see you're hurting." Marie softened her tone and looked into his eyes. "I can take care of you here just fine." She ran the back of her index finger down the length of his cheek.

Raul held her gaze and took hold of her wrist. "I've missed this, Marie. I've missed us."

"Things haven't been the same since we got back from Japan, have they?"

Bringing her hand to his lips, he placed a lingering kiss on her fingers. The touch of her skin sent ripples of fire coursing through his veins. "Let's go back to the way things were. You know, back when we were care-free. Life was good."

Marie tore her eyes away and dropped her gaze, slipping her wrist out of his grasp. Though she only pulled back a few inches, it felt like a canyon existed between them. Raul waited for her response, but the only sound filling the space between them came from the waves as they crashed on the shore. Each briny surge crushed his heart a little bit more than the one before it as the silence stretched on. What had he done wrong to make her pull away like this? This wasn't the Marie he knew.

"I'd better get to work on that foot." She spoke without lifting her eyes to meet his.

Raul forced a weak smile and nodded as Marie rushed toward the back door. He didn't have much time to think before she returned with a first aid kit and a couple of bottles of water.

"Thanks, I'm parched," he said.

"These aren't for drinking. I need these to wash your foot out." Marie opened the kit and pulled out the supplies she needed.

"Where did you find that?"

"This is an old kit I had lying around the house. I thought it might come in handy and packed it in the basket."

Raul tilted his head, trying to catch Marie's eyes, but she busied herself about her work. "Marie—"

"Hold on, this might hurt."

A bolt of pain shot through Raul's foot a moment later. He groaned and puffed his cheeks, trying to get a handle on himself. "Whoa! You weren't kidding. What did you do?"

Marie lifted tweezers into the air, triumphantly displaying the offending shard of glass. "That was one nasty hunk of glass. I just need to clean out the cut, bandage you up, and you'll be good as new."

"I don't know about that."

"It looks like a pretty clean cut. It shouldn't have any trouble healing up nicely." She opened one of the bottles of water and poured it over the cut, its clear stream washing away the sand caught inside.

"I'm not talking about the cut, Marie. What's going on with us? How can I be as good as new when I can feel you pulling away from me?" He missed what they once had, and it was tearing him up inside.

Marie looked him in the eyes for the first time since the change had come over her. "It's not you I'm pulling away from—it's this whole situation. She knows, Raul. Somehow Meg knows about us."

"I never told her a thing," Raul said.

"I think there are some things that don't have to be told."

"Have you ever wondered if your fear of the media might be a little out of proportion? What's the worst thing that could happen if Meg finds out about us?"

"First of all, it's not a fear. I don't like the idea of attention from the media. It would be different if we were married, but you know what tabloids are like. They try to turn everything into some kind of nasty scandal. I just can't deal with that on a personal or professional level."

"Yeah, but I have a say in what's broadcast on the show." Raul said.

"Did you forget about Meg's tabloid?"

Raul didn't have a good reply. Marie was right. One false step and Meg wouldn't hesitate to publish a story on the two of them, whether it was a true story or not. "So where does that leave us?"

Marie was silent for several seconds as she chewed the inside of her cheek. She placed a square of gauze on his foot and taped it in place, running her fingers lightly over the adhesive strips. "I think we need to lie low for a while."

"Good plan. That's exactly what we're doing."

"No. *Really* low," Marie said.

"Meaning what?"

Marie fiddled with the large butterfly ring on her right middle-finger, refusing to look up into his eyes. "I don't think we should see each other for a while."

A cold chill wracked Raul's body, sending icy prickles up and down the length of his spine. "Like for a week?"

"I don't know." Marie shook her head, swirling her toe in the sand. "Maybe longer?"

He stiffened as the hairs on the back of his neck stood on end. "I don't think I like the direction this is heading. Are you saying you want to break up with me?"

Marie's eyes shot up to meet Raul's gaze. "No, that's

not what I want at all. I just think we need to play it extra safe. I don't think we should see each other until you're done filming the show."

Raul's breath hitched in his throat. "That could be another three months, at least." This was the biggest mess he'd ever made, and things were getting messier by the minute. He'd left the racing circuit so he could spend more time with Marie. What had he been thinking signing up for a reality TV show?

If he hadn't been so wrapped up in his own problems, he'd have been able to see that inviting a camera crew to follow his every move would be more than a little uncomfortable for Marie. The very thing that was supposed to save him from being alone with his own thoughts was destroying the only thing he truly valued—his relationship with the woman he loved.

"I think this is the only way to keep our relationship out of the limelight," Marie said.

It was also the best way he could think of to kill what they had together. But as much as he hated to admit it, he couldn't think of a better solution.

Marie sat next to him on the stair and interlaced her fingers with his. "I hate the idea too, but we can still text and face-time every day."

"Yeah, we'll do that." Raul's voice sounded like it was on autopilot as he wrapped his arm around her shoulder. "Let's try to enjoy what's left of the day. I guess this is the last time we'll be together for a while."

He leaned down and placed a soft kiss on the top of her head, wondering how long it would actually be before he smelled the sweet fragrance of her hair again. His stomach twisted into a knot. Keeping their relationship a secret may have been the absolute worst idea he'd ever come up with.

Fourteen

The late afternoon sun streamed in through the brand new window of Marie's freshly renovated office at Williams Elementary. Even the tiny flecks of dust floating in and out of the sunbeam illuminating her desk seemed nicer than the old dust that used to share the office with her.

The smell of fresh paint hung in the air, reminding her of the night she'd met Raul at the fundraiser for her struggling inner-city school. They'd raised more than enough money that night to purchase the new text books and updated tech the children needed, with plenty to spare for some much-needed renovations on the aging building.

She picked up the framed photo of her and Raul from the corner of her desk. It was a picture from their first date: brunch at a local deli. It was so un-billionaire-ish of him to take her to a mom and pop joint on a street corner. He'd been irresistible the evening before with his dazzling smile and boundless charm, but that day, at the sandwich shop, she'd gotten a good long look at the real him. That was when she knew she could fall hard for him, given the opportunity. The months that followed that first date had given her plenty of opportunities, and she'd proven herself right. She was in love.

She traced the line of Raul's masculine jaw in the photo. A stab of regret pierced her heart at the sensation of the cool, smooth glass beneath her fingertip. She ached to feel the rugged warmth of his stubbly chin, and run her fingers through his wavy black hair.

It had been weeks since their last day together on the beach. Phone calls were a poor replacement for actual time spent together. She missed him more than she had known it was possible to miss another human being. She'd questioned her decision to stay away from Raul more than a few times lately, but none more so than now. She had reached her breaking point and didn't know how much longer she could handle this secret relationship. It wasn't working.

Raul may have been right. Had she blown the idea of the media knowing about their relationship out of proportion? The thought of being portrayed as a billionaire's female flavor of the month in the tabloids had been a very real fear for her when they first started dating. Perhaps it was time to stop worrying about other people's perceptions, and go after the life she wanted.

She looked around at the stacks of paperwork on her desk. The school year was still young and she hadn't settled into a good routine yet. There was so much work to be done, but she didn't have the heart to dive into it. Glancing at the clock on the wall, she rolled her eyes and sighed. She still had half of an hour to kill before it was time to pick up Sam from his after-school soccer camp.

She drummed her fingers, skimming through uninteresting pages filled with classroom assignments and teacher duty schedules. It made for dry reading on the best of days, but it was torturous on a day like today. All she wanted to do was escape those four walls and drive straight to Raul's home.

She knew exactly what she'd do when she got there. She'd waltz right up to him, throw her arms around his neck, and plant a toe curling kiss on his lips. Who cared who knew about them? They'd weather any media storm together and come out on the other side stronger than before.

Marie jumped at a knock on her door. Bonnie, the head secretary, popped her head into the office. She tucked a stray tendril of brown hair tinged with silver behind her ear—all natural wisdom highlights, as she liked to call them. "There's someone here to see you, Marie." Her brown eyes sparkled as the soft pink apples of her cheeks drew up into a smile laced with both excitement and mystery. Pulling her glasses down to the end of her nose, she looked over the top rim. Ever the hopeful matchmaker, she wiggled her brows up and down. "It's a gentleman," she said.

Marie's stomach leapt into her throat. Raul! "Send him in, Bonnie. Send him in."

Marie grabbed a handful of her thick hair and pulled it forward over her shoulder, smoothing it down several times with both hands. Forcing herself to take deep breaths, she stood to adjust her clothes. It looked like she wouldn't have to make that drive out to Raul's place this evening, after all.

"Go right on in," Bonnie said.

The sound of her voice sent a thrill racing through Marie's body. Suddenly petrified that she might have lipstick smudged on her front teeth, she lunged for her purse and dug out her compact mirror. Turning her back to the door, she rubbed furiously at her front teeth with her index finger.

All at once, the smell of paint combined with the musky scent of a man's cologne and filled the room. The masculine aroma sent her senses into a whirl. This was something new. She'd never known Raul to wear musk, but she was liking it. Honestly, she wouldn't have cared if he smelled like a dead fish. All she wanted to do was be near him again.

A smile that she couldn't bottle up stretched from ear to ear as she spun around to greet her visitor. Every thought and emotion she'd had in the last thirty seconds came to a screeching halt. Where she expected to see Raul's lean, muscled frame and bronzed skin, stood a man with a protruding belly and sunburnt arms.

Confusion swirled in her mind as her cheeks burned with embarrassment. What had she been thinking? There hadn't been any reason to expect Raul would visit her.

The man standing in front of her looked vaguely familiar, with his long blond hair pulled back in a low ponytail. But the crushing disappointment of seeing him stand in for Raul made it difficult to clear her mind enough to think straight.

"How can I help you?" The words formed in her mouth without any help from her conscious mind.

He stepped up to the desk and set a small canvas bag down, adjusting its angle several times before he was satisfied enough to sit down himself. He tugged on the bill of the well-worn, army-green ball cap on his head. Though the word had nearly faded away, she could still read what was printed on the hat. *Smile.*

Marie gasped; she'd seen that hat before.

The man reached out to shake her hand, but she shied away as if he had the plague. "You're that camera man from Raul's show," she said.

"The name is Miles. I was hoping you'd remember me." He flashed a hopeful smile.

Marie struggled to put on a more professional demeanor. She gritted her teeth and pasted a smile back on her face—a decidedly less enthusiastic one. "How could I forget. Why are you here at my school? Shouldn't you be off filming Raul?"

"I usually would be, but it's my day off. I'm only interested in you today."

Marie held up her hands and sat at her desk. "No, thank you. I'm not interested. I've made it clear how I feel about the show." She pulled a stack of papers out of her bottom drawer and busied herself with going through them, pretending to look for something of great importance.

Miles slid his chair closer to the desk. "Oh, this isn't about Raul's show. Meg has no idea I'm here, and I'd like to keep it that way, too, if it's all right with you."

Marie leaned forward, resting her elbows on her desk. "Your secret is safe with me. I don't have any contact with her."

The tension in Miles's shoulders melted away at Marie's words. "You don't know how good it is to hear you say that. If she knew what I was up to, I'd be out of work by the end of the day."

"Well, that sounds ominous." Marie's brows drew together. She didn't trust any colleague of Meg Monroe's, but she couldn't deny the curiosity brewing deep inside. "What *are* you up to?"

"I'm trying to break out of the rat race. Filming reality TV shows is only my day job. What I really am at the heart, is an indie film maker. I want to do something with my talent. You know, change the world kind of stuff."

"Why can't Meg know that?"

"She's an all-or-nothing kind of person. If she finds out I've got a side-gig going on, she'll drop me like a bad habit." Miles leaned back in his chair, tilting his hat up to scratch his scalp underneath.

"That's all pretty interesting, but it still doesn't tell me why you're sitting in my office."

"I need your help."

Marie splayed her palms on the desk, doing her best to plaster a no-nonsense look on her face. "I'm not interested in appearing in any—"

"I'm not asking you to appear in anything. I want to make a big splash at the spring film festival with a hard-hitting piece on our failing school system. You seem to have single-handedly turned this school around. I was hoping you could be my 'unnamed source'. I want to make sure I've got my facts straight, and what better place is there to get the facts than from someone in your position?"

Marie narrowed her eyes, slowly shaking her head as she considered what Miles was asking her to do. "I don't know, Miles."

"It would help me out so much. And think about how much good something like this could do. Do you have any idea how many people a film like this could inspire?"

Miles had a point. The fundraiser had provided a huge boost for her school. They had really thought outside the box when planning it, and the superintendent intended to hold similar events for other schools in the district in the future. Their district was going to be fine, but what about other struggling schools across the country? It would be selfish not to spread the message of how she'd helped pull her school out of the gutter.

She bit down on her bottom lip. "I wouldn't be in the film—at all?"

"Not at all."

"All right. I'll do what I can to help."

Miles shot out of his chair and stretched his hand across the desk to shake Marie's. "I'll put together a coherent list of interview questions for you. Can I call you to set up a time for us to get together and chat?"

"Yeah, here's my card."

Miles stuck the card in his shirt pocket and headed toward the door. He spun on his heels, pointing at Marie with both index fingers. "It's gonna be great." He drummed on the door jamb and stepped into the outer office, leaving his bag sitting on Marie's desk.

She grabbed it and hurried after him. "You forgot this." She tossed it to him across the main reception desk.

Wide-eyed, Miles scrambled to catch it. He snatched it out of the air as delicately as if there were a dozen raw eggs inside. "Th-thanks." His lips curled into an awkward smile as he unzipped the bag and checked on its contents. "I wouldn't want to forget this."

Bonnie stood and reached for her purse. "I'm ready to close up shop for the day. How about you, Marie?"

"You read my mind." Marie took her belongings from the cubby along the wall and locked her office door. Excitement danced in the pit of her stomach as she led the way out of the office and down the hall toward the main exit. She'd made her decision. She couldn't wait to see the look on Raul's face when she showed up on his doorstep.

"It's amazing what a fresh coat of paint did to brighten these halls," Bonnie said.

Marie glanced behind her as she rounded a corner. "It's like the difference between night and—" Her words were cut short when she walked into a man, one of his big hands taking hold of her arm to steady her from the surprise. Her jaw fell open when her eyes fell on the very person she hadn't been able to get out of her mind all day. Raul.

"Hello," he said, the rich baritone timber of his voice causing the breath to catch in her throat. The eagerness in his eyes betrayed his calm tone. He was just as excited as she was.

"H-hello."

"Mr. De Luca? What are you doing here?" Miles said.

Raul cut his eyes to where Miles stood and immediately released Marie's arm. Shock filled his eyes as he took a step back. "I could ask you the same thing."

"I came by to ask for Miss Maranzano's help on a project I'm working on."

Raul's brows raised before lowering into a furrowed scowl. "A project? I hope you're not pressuring my friends to do anything they don't want to do." His voice was an octave lower than Marie had ever heard it before. Its protective tone released a wave of butterflies into her stomach.

"I'm only helping with the information he needs to make the film a success," Marie said.

"And you're okay with this?" Raul said.

"Yes, I've been assured that I won't appear on camera—at all."

Raul eyed Miles with suspicion, his chest expanded to its full capacity.

"Please don't tell Meg," Miles pleaded.

"Keep your end of the bargain and you won't have any trouble from me." Looking back at Marie, Raul said, "I hope I didn't hurt you just now, Miss Maranzano."

"Not at all," Marie said. "Are your flowers okay?" Her heart danced despite the formal tone he'd put on for Miles's sake. Not only had he come to see her, he'd brought her favorite flowers.

Raul held up a bundle of soft-pink carnations, inspecting them with a critical eye. "I think they survived."

"What *are* you doing here?" She asked the question, but her heart was certain she already knew the answer. He couldn't stay away from her any more than she could stay away from him.

"I was in the neighborhood and wanted to stop by to let you know that I... uh..." He hesitated, as if he were trying to pull his answer out of the air around him. "I'm leaving for Miami for a while, and I won't be available to discuss our school program for the next few weeks."

Marie's spirits fell. Miami? So much for her grand plans of making things right, and spending every spare moment with him. She couldn't bring herself to look him in the eyes. "Thank you for letting me know."

"What a gorgeous bouquet of flowers," Bonnie said.

"I'm glad you like them," Raul said, his eyes flicking over to Miles for a fraction of a second before refocusing on Bonnie. "They're for you. It *is* Secretary's Day, right?"

"Nope, but I'll accept flowers on any day of the year. So sweet of you to think of me," she said.

Marie caught sight of Raul palming the card out of the bouquet and sliding it into his pocket. A defeated sigh escaped her lips. That was the second bouquet of flowers meant for her that went to another woman instead. She just couldn't seem to catch a break lately.

Bonnie buried her nose in the bouquet and inhaled deeply. "There must be two dozen carnations here. This is the best Secretary's Day bouquet I've ever gotten. Thank you."

"Of course," Raul said, rubbing his hand along the back of his neck.

The four of them headed toward the glass doors at the

end of the hall. Marie wondered if the silence felt as awkward to anyone else as it did to her. Glancing around, she saw Bonnie happily admiring her bouquet, Miles seemingly preoccupied with his bag, and Raul walking along with an unreadable expression on his face. Marie seemed to be the only one who felt out of place in the silence.

When they stepped outside and into the light, Raul paused and offered Marie his hand. "I guess I'll see you in a few weeks."

She gazed up into his dark-brown eyes, every fiber of her being aching to wrap her arms around him and never let him go. Her mind screamed, 'Don't go!' but her mouth couldn't seem to form the words. Instead she reached out, her heart fluttering at the way his large hand enveloped hers with a gentleness she'd never known from another man.

"I'll look forward to seeing you when you get back," Marie said.

She blinked back her tears of disappointment, and forced herself to take one last look into his eyes. She searched for a message hidden in their depths—a hint of the same eagerness she'd spied in them before. All she needed was a sign that he hated their separation as much as she did, but she found none. He was playing his part well. If he was still on board with their plan and willing to keep up their charade, she would play along too.

The warmth of his touch evaporated the moment he released her hand and headed for his car. A bone-chilling cold crept up her arm and came to rest in her heart as she watched him drive away without looking back. If this arrangement was killing him on the inside as much as it was her, he was doing a good job of hiding it—a very good job.

Fifteen

Raul sat on the glossy bench of the baby grand in his Miami penthouse hotel room. He stared out the wall of windows to his left at the waves crashing on South Beach. The last rays of the sun bathed the sand in hues of coral and pink. It would have been the perfect view to share with Marie.

"She would have loved it here." He heaved a heavy sigh and muttered the words beneath his breath.

Brushing his fingers over the antique ivory keys, he wished he had paid better attention during his piano lessons as a child. It would have felt good to play a soulful lover's ballad to soothe his aching heart. Why had he given up so easily at the school the other day? He'd gone there to throw caution to the wind and profess his undying love to the woman of his dreams once and for all. But the sight of one greasy-faced cameraman had shaken his confidence.

If only Miles hadn't been there. It would have been wrong to out their secret right in front of one of the very people they'd agreed to keep it from, wouldn't it? Yes, it would have been all wrong. But why didn't he go to Marie's house later that night? He'd done nothing but make one poor decision after another lately, and the thought of what it might cost him kept him up at night.

He raked his fingers through his hair, tugging on the ends in frustration. He'd left Marie—and his heart—back in New York. All he felt now was empty and alone.

"Are you listening to a word I'm saying to you?" The abrasive tone of Meg's voice was like sandpaper to Raul's ears, rubbing him in all the wrong ways.

"It seems like you're saying the same words over and over again. It all starts to run together after a while, you know?" Raul pecked out a rough rendition of chopsticks, watching Meg out of the corner of his eye.

She sighed and tossed her head, her chemically-burnt blond hair barely reacting with any motion at all. The crow's feet on either side of her eyes stretched and warped as she massaged her temples. "All I'm saying is that I need more from you. We're in South Beach, for crying out loud. You're the most eligible bachelor on the Eastern seaboard. The party is going on down there." She gestured out the window toward an outdoor concert happening on the beach. "Yet, here you are. Staying in. Again."

"You said you wanted the real me. What you see is what you get. Besides, my foot still hurts." Raul shrugged without turning his head in Meg's direction.

"Don't give me that lame excuse about your foot again. You walk on it whenever *you* want to." She motioned toward him with outstretched arms. "*This*, whatever it is, is not the man I followed in the media for the last ten years. You've always been impulsive, exciting, irresponsible. That's the man I signed to a reality television deal."

"All you've done for the last few weeks is try to push me into the party scene. I'm not that guy any more. You said you didn't want to produce a run-of-the-mill reality show. You wanted to make a documentary of my life. Well, this is it. Document it."

"Who do you think you're kidding? You didn't actually believe me when I said we were going to be filming a documentary. You're smarter than that. You signed up for a reality television series. Everyone knows what that means."

"Oh, really?" A discordant sound gushed from the piano when Raul turned and leaned on the keys, glaring at Meg with furrowed brows. "What does it mean?"

"It means you need to live a life worth watching, Raul. Nobody wants to tune in to a reality show called 'The Sulking Billionaire'—it's boring. A lot is riding on this show."

He spun the rest of the way around on the polished surface of the piano bench, holding Meg's gaze. "What? What is riding on it? It isn't going to rock my world if nobody watches. I don't care if the show tanks."

"My career is hanging in the balance." The momentary look of horror and surprise that flashed across Meg's features at the shrill words that had flown out of her mouth was almost enough to make Raul pity her. With flushed cheeks, she continued in a softer tone. "If this show doesn't get the ratings I promised my boss, I'm gone."

"You should have thought of that before you signed me under false pretenses."

The dedicated elevator for Raul's penthouse chimed, announcing the soon arrival of a guest.

"If you'll excuse me, I'm expecting an old friend. You should take the night off, because I'm not going to give you what you want tonight—or ever."

Meg's jaw flapped up and down with all the grace of an albatross trying to take flight before she clamped her mouth shut. The muscles on either side of her jaw flexed wildly as she stood with her arms crossed over her chest, her narrowed gaze burning a hole into him. "I have the power to make your life miserable, you know."

"You can't threaten me with something you've already done." Though his tone was brave, his pulse quickened at her menacing words. He couldn't help but wonder if she was referring to her Internet tabloid.

The elevator doors opened, revealing a friendly face.

"Jonas," Raul said.

Jonas stepped out of the elevator. He wore a pair of stylish loafers without socks and a pastel blazer over a designer t-shirt. "Sorry, am I early? I can come back later if you need me to," he said.

"No, Meg was just leaving." Raul shot the television producer a stern look. "I just gave her the night off."

Meg stormed past Jonas, stomping into the elevator and disappearing behind its automated doors.

"Whoa," said Jonas. "What did I walk into?"

"Nothing. She's just having a meltdown because she's not getting her way. But what's up with you, man? You look like you just walked off the set of that old 80's TV cop show."

"Well, we are in Miami, after all." Jonas's laughter sounded strained. His pale complexion highlighted the dark circles beneath both eyes. He'd looked tired the last time Raul had seen him, but this time he looked unwell.

"Thanks for coming over, man," said Raul. "I'd hoped you could help me sort some things out, but you look like you've been put through the wringer yourself. Is everything okay?" Raul hadn't seen Jonas look so bad since their days of pulling all-nighters when they were building the tech company that made them and their college buddies all billionaires.

"It's just business. It takes its toll. But I'm fine. I'm here to liquidate some assets that should take a little bit of pressure off—so it's all good. What's up with you? You didn't sound like yourself over the phone."

The two men headed for the overstuffed furniture decorating the open floor plan of the room.

"I'm miserable, man. Miserable," Raul said.

"What are you doing in Miami?" Jonas asked.

"I just told you. I'm here being miserable."

"Then do something about it."

Raul plopped down on one of the couches. "What do you mean?"

"I mean it's time to take charge. You've sat back and let life happen to you ever since your dad died. That's not the Raul I met all those years ago back in college. It's not the son your father raised. If you don't like what's going on in your life, change it."

No one had ever called him out like that before. If Jonas had spoken those very same words to him only a month sooner, Raul wouldn't have been ready to hear them. But something was different tonight. The stakes were higher. His future with Marie was on the line.

It was time to take charge of his life, but there were still a few pieces of the puzzle that he had no control over.

"There are some things I can't change. Marie is still fostering," Raul said.

"Raul, you're my best friend. I hope you can hear the heart behind what I'm about to tell you. I know you can't put grief and healing on a timeline, but I think it's time for you to start taking some steps toward recovery. You need to find a way to get past what happened to your dad so you can go after Marie with everything you've got."

"You don't just get past something like that, Jonas. You know what I did. It was my money that bought the ultra-light. It's my fault he's dead."

"What happened to your dad was tragic, but it wasn't your fault. It was an accident. Your father didn't put his heart into raising you so you could live your life in mourning. You're his legacy—the part of him he expected to continue *living* long after he was gone."

Raul's heart pounded in his ears as Jonas's words soaked into his heart.

"Grief and regret is no way to live, Raul. Your father wouldn't have wanted it for you."

Raul sat in silence for a few moments as ten years of haze lifted from his mind. He was seeing things clearly for the first time in ages. Jonas was right. It was time to make a change. "How do you do it?"

Jonas quirked a brow. "Do what?"

"How do you always know exactly what to say?"

"It's a gift." Jonas took a comical bow before a sober expression came over his face. "That package your dad sent you has been sitting in my closet for too long. I'm going to call my man back in Chicago and have it delivered to your new place in New York. Just promise me that you'll give opening it some serious thought when you get home."

Raul swallowed hard. Jonas had been the keeper of the last remnants of his relationship with his father for many years. If he was ever going to heal and move on from the past, he needed to quit hiding from it. Now was the time.

"You're right, man. It's time I finally open it and see what's in the box. It wasn't easy having that package arrive after the funeral. I guess I kind of freaked. I knew once I found out what he'd sent, that would be the last time I'd ever hear from him again. I just couldn't deal with it. But you're right, it's time."

"It's a good first step in the right direction, but what else are you going to do?" Jonas stared at Raul, waiting for a reply.

"What else?"

"You're in love with Marie, but she's in New York..." He looked hard at Raul, waiting for the full effect of his words to sink in. "And you're in Miami."

Raul leapt to his feet as a bolt of excitement shot through his body. "I know exactly what I'm going to do. I'm going to have my lawyer get me out of this television deal, get on my jet, and fly back to Marie." He sprinted to the bedroom to pack his things.

"What's your rush?" Jonas laughed, following him out of the room. "It's too late to do anything tonight. Why don't you give her a call?"

Raul had already emptied the top two drawers of the ebony dresser opposite the bed, and was on his way back to his suitcase with another armful of clothing before Jonas made it to the door. He froze mid-stride and looked up as Jonas entered the room. "No. No phone calls. This is big. Life changing. I've got to have a face-to-face with her. She deserves it."

He knew they wouldn't arrive in New York until the wee hours of the morning that night, but he couldn't sit still and do nothing for another moment. Tomorrow was going to be epic. He was going to sweep Marie off her feet so hard they might never touch the ground again.

SIXTEEN

Marie sat at her kitchen table, staring at the laptop in front of her. The cool early morning breeze filtering in through an open window was balanced by the sun's warmth as its rays beat down on her back.

A quarter of a pot of coffee still sat on the warming plate of her coffee maker, its smell sweetened by the lingering aroma of a breakfast pastry Sam had heated up in the microwave a few minutes before. It was the perfect lazy Saturday morning.

A quiet smile spread across her face as Sam's laughter met her ears. Listening to him giggle at his morning cartoons had quickly become one of the highlight of Marie's days. She'd never realized just how empty her house had been until Sam came along.

Despite her idyllic surroundings, she couldn't seem to get comfortable in her seat. Ants in her pants—that's what her mother would have called it. She couldn't sit still as she scrolled through the results of her most recent Internet search: adoption laws in the state of New York.

She chewed the tip of one of her fingernails, clicking between the open tabs of her Internet browser. She'd found a wealth of information that morning and now it was time to sift through it and try to make sense of it all. There was so much to learn.

Marie leaned back in her chair, tilted her head up, and gazed at the popcorn ceiling above her. The phone call she'd received from Sam's case worker earlier that week had been a wake-up call. It was time to make some big decisions.

She'd gone into fostering assuming that her home would become a safe haven for a steady stream of children as they transitioned through some of the most difficult times in their young lives. But now that Sam's situation was changing, Marie knew in her heart it was time for her plans to change as well.

Nothing had ever shocked her more than the news that his mother had signed away all of her parental rights. According to the caseworker, it wasn't unheard of for parents facing the certainty of hard time to sign their children over into state custody in hopes of them being placed in permanent homes. Although Marie recognized it as the ultimate act of love, she still couldn't wrap her mind around someone being able to willingly give up all claim to such an amazing child.

Marie closed her eyes, savoring the memory of the first night she had really connected with Sam. It was late in the evening, and she'd stripped his bed so he could have a fresh set of sheets to crawl into after his shower.

Sam watched her intently from the door as she tugged the fitted sheet into place.

"That looks hard," he said.

"It takes a little bit of muscle, but I'll get it."

He wandered into the room and stood at the other side of the bed. "Why do you do all this stuff?"

"What stuff?"

"You put blankets on the bed. You cook all the time. You always wash my clothes."

"It's what moms do, sweetie. I know I'm only your foster mom, but I love taking good care of you."

"My mom never did anything."

Marie remembered the silence that had followed. She hadn't known what to say. She'd had the benefit of growing up with an amazing and caring mother and couldn't possibly imagine what life must have been like for Sam before he came to live with her.

He slowly made his way around the foot of the bed to stand by her side. "Marie, can I pretend you're my real mom while I'm here?"

Tears pricked her eyes the moment the words came out of his mouth. She cleared her throat to dislodge the knot in it. "Of course you can, sweetie."

"Okay," was his only reply before skipping out of the room to get cleaned up for the night.

Marie shifted in her kitchen chair and placed her chin on her palm. A dreamy smile rested on her lips as the warmth from that night flooded her heart again. She had cared deeply for Sam from the first moment he'd walked through her door, but it was that night in his bedroom that he had found his way into her heart forever.

She couldn't imagine a life where she wasn't the one caring for him—protecting him. He needed a good family and a strong mother to love him unconditionally throughout the rest of his life. And Marie was ready to charge full-steam ahead to give that to him.

She took a deep breath as she refocused on the laptop.

Her clumsy fingers vibrated with nervous energy as she fumbled through various web pages, trying to figure out where to start reading first. Visions of a future together as mother and son bombarded her mind, making it nearly impossible to concentrate.

The unmistakable rumble of Raul's sports car pulling into the driveway sent a thrill racing through her. She shot to her feet and raced to the window. Her chest rose and fell with rapid shallow breaths. The giddy quivering of her stomach and her weak knees reminded her of one thing—she was hopelessly in love with the man exiting the canary yellow car in her driveway.

She glanced down at her outfit. At least one of the colors in her tie-dyed leggings coordinated with the oversized t-shirt she'd paired it with. It wasn't her best look, but who cared what she was wearing? She wasn't about to waste time changing into a fresh outfit. Not when those were precious moments she could spend wrapped in Raul's strong arms.

Unable to contain herself another moment, she raced out the side door and met him halfway down the driveway. With a smile so wide it threatened to crack her face, she stretched to her full height and threw her arms around his neck. He pulled her close, gazing at her with wildfire dancing in his eyes that heated her body to the core.

"What are you doing here? I thought you were in Miami," Marie said.

"I couldn't stay away."

His husky voice sent a ripple of excitement coursing through her veins. Raul wove his fingers into the thick hair at the base of her neck and drew her face close to his. Marie's breath caught in her throat as every inch of her body waited to be kissed by the man she'd missed so desperately.

Raul leaned down and rested his forehead against hers. "All I want to do is hold you close and never let go."

"Sounds good to me." Marie placed her hand on his broad chest, breathing in time with the rhythm of his beating heart.

He took a sudden deep breath and stepped back, holding her at arm's length. "Marie, I've got so much to say to you. I've been practicing it ever since I got in at four this morning. I've got to say it now, before anything else happens."

Marie looked into the depths of his eyes, a flirtatious smile tugging on her lips. "Even before I get my hello kiss?"

A deep growl of a laugh rolled around at the back of his throat. "Especially before then." He traced a finger along the edge of her lower lip. "Once these lips touch mine, my brain is going to be about as useful as a bowl full of fruit gelatin."

Marie grabbed his hand and tugged him toward the door. "Well, let's get in the house and get talking so we can hurry up and say a proper 'hello'."

The screen door clattered behind them as they hurried into the kitchen. Marie sat in her seat and pushed the chair across from her out with her foot. "I saved you a seat." Her heart thundered in her ears as Raul sat.

Resting his elbows on the table, he stretched his arms out with his palms turned upward, inviting Marie to take his hands. She shoved her laptop out of the way and placed her hands in his, tingles racing up her arms at his touch. Her eyelashes fluttered at the intensity of his gaze. Whatever he had to say, he'd better make it quick. She didn't know how much longer she'd be able to stay on her side of the table.

"These past few weeks have been all wrong, and I'm the only one to blame for it. I'm quitting the show, Marie. My lawyer is on the job right now. All I want is to be with you. I'm willing to wait for you to finish up with your commitments. I don't care how long I have to wait, as long as I know you're going to be a part of my future."

Marie's brows drew together as a confused smile curved her lips into a question. "What commitments? I don't have anything going on that would keep me from you."

"Well, you know—" Raul stopped talking when Sam entered the room.

Marie quickly spun the laptop around to keep the boy from catching a glimpse of her research. Raul's eyes widened when he came face-to-face with the screen. She cringed as she placed her hand back in his. She'd sprung the idea of becoming a foster mother on him without warning. This wasn't how she'd wanted him to find out about her intent to adopt.

"Hey, Raul," Sam said, on his way to the refrigerator.

"Lookin' good, Sam. I think you've grown an inch since I saw you at the beach." The stiffness in Raul's suddenly clammy hands betrayed more than his voice did as he gazed at Sam with an unreadable expression on his face.

"Maybe." Sam cracked open an ice-cold bottle of pineapple-orange juice and chugged half of it down before heading back to the living room. "You guys can go ahead and start kissing again. I'm done in here."

Marie's cheeks burned. "Oh, honey, we weren't kissing."

Sam paused in the doorway, looking at them with a grin

on his face. "But you know you want to." He smothered his giggles in his juice bottle as he hurried back to his cartoon.

Marie squeezed her eyes shut and sucked in a deep breath. "Before you say anything, let me just say..." Her mind was a complete blank. She had no idea how to break the news to him—she hadn't thought that far ahead yet.

"Adoption?" Raul's brows sat high on his forehead.

Marie raised a finger to her lips, signaling Raul to lower his voice. Mouthing the words with hardly any voice, she said, "Let's take this outside."

A few moments after closing the lid of her laptop, she found herself back in the open air, standing in her driveway. Sighing one final time to quiet her nerves, she looked up at Raul. "Yes, adoption. Sam doesn't know it yet, but his mother signed away her parental rights earlier this week. Now he can be adopted into a forever family."

Raul took Marie by the arms, a huge smile lighting up every feature of his face. "That's fantastic. It's better than fantastic—it's perfect! Once he's adopted, he'll be taken care of, and you'll be all done fostering." Wrapping her in his arms once again, he pulled her close. "Everything is falling into place for us."

Raul moved in for a kiss, but for the first time, Marie wasn't interested. She placed a hand on his chest and pulled back. "Yeah, he'll be taken care of. I'll be taking care of him."

"Of course you will, I get that. He's your responsibility until someone adopts him. I assume it's probably a pretty long process, but once it's all over, it'll be just you and me again." Coming in for a second try, he breathed the words hot on her lips, "You're the only baby I'll ever need."

Marie broke the circle of his arms around her, and

stepped back. "*Someone* isn't going to adopt him, Raul." She swallowed hard. "I'm going to adopt him."

Raul's jaw dropped as all of the color drained from his stunned face.

Something inside compelled Marie to fill the silence that stretched between them. "There's still a lot to learn on my end, but that's the direction I'm moving in, at least. I didn't plan on telling you like this. I mean, I didn't know how I was going to tell you, but this is something I've got to do."

Raul stood still, gazing at her with a blank look in his eyes.

"You understand that, right?" she said. "I have to do it."

Her last words seemed to free his tongue.

"But you can't adopt him. You wanted to be a foster parent. That's a temporary situation. Temporary. Nothing about this was supposed to last." He raked his fingers through his hair and paced in a tight circle in front of her. "Marie, I've been waiting all this time for you to finish up with this whole idea of fostering so we can move on with our lives."

Marie couldn't believe what she was hearing. Was this the same man she'd seen laughing and playing with Sam as he taught him how to paddle board? "Listen to yourself, Raul. You don't 'finish up' with a child who needs you. His mother has just signed him away. She gave him up. Do you have any idea what something like that does to a child? He has no one!"

"He'll have a new family who loves him after the adoption," Raul said.

"I love him." Marie pounded on her heart with a clenched fist as the passionate words resonated in her own ears.

"Don't you love me?"

Her heart dropped into her stomach at the simple question. She'd never heard his voice sound so small and uncertain. Of course she loved him. She loved him more than she'd ever loved any man before—more than she could ever love anyone else in the future. How could he question that?

"You know I do. But you saw him just now. Sam's thriving here. He's not even the same kid who came to live with me back in August. I can't turn my back on him now."

"But you can you turn your back on me?"

"That's not fair, Raul. I'm not turning my back on you."

"But I've told you I can't be a father. Now here you are talking about adopting?"

"That's what you say, but every time you and Sam are together, you're amazing with him."

Beads of sweat formed on his forehead. "That's not being a father, Marie."

"I'm not asking you to be a father." Marie's breath hitched in her throat. "Unless you're saying that you want to marry me?"

"That's always been my end game. Didn't you know? I love you Marie, but I can't be a father."

"Why not?"

He gazed into her eyes. The pain she saw in their depths made her heart ache for him.

His arms hung limp at his sides. "I don't even know where to begin. I hadn't counted on talking about this today."

"I'm not asking for a speech, Raul. Just a simple explanation."

"That's just it. There is no simple explanation. It's something I've never talked about. Ever. I need you to trust me. Trust that I love you. That I want to give you the world. You're asking me for the one thing I'm not able to give you." He cut his eyes away, but not before she saw the tears filling them.

Marie's head swam as her own stinging tears blurred the world around her. A bottleneck of stifled sobs created a painful knot in her throat. "Everyone else in his life has abandoned him." Her quivering voice strained against the words. "I can't do it to him, too."

The long silence that followed tore at her heart, ruthlessly clawing away at every hope and dream she'd stored up since the night she'd met her prince charming.

Without lifting his gaze from the cement at his feet, Raul whispered, "I guess there's nothing more to say."

"I guess not." Marie clamped a hand over her mouth as she watched Raul walk to the driver's side door and disappear into his car as if in a daze. The engine roared to life. She wanted to call out to him, but he was right. There wasn't anything more that could be said. They loved each other, there was no question about that, but they stood on opposite sides of an impassable gulf.

She pressed her back against the aluminum siding of her home to steady her shaky limbs as his car backed onto the street and rolled out of sight. She slowly slid to the ground, listening to the sound of his engine grow fainter by the moment, her shoulders quaking with unvoiced sobs.

There she sat for several minutes, tears flowing freely down her cheeks, until she heard Sam calling from inside. Scrambling to her feet, she used the bottom of her t-shirt to wipe her face dry just before Sam stepped outside.

"Someone's been blowing your phone up." He held her phone out to her.

Marie sniffed. "Thank you, sweetheart."

Sam's green eyes clouded over. "Are you all right?"

"I'm fine, sweetie." She stepped up to him and draped her arm around his shoulders. Pulling him into a quick hug, she kissed the top of his head. "I do sound a little stuffy, don't I?" She spoke with as light of a tone as she could muster, doing everything she could to shield the boy from the heartache she felt inside.

Her phone went off again as they stepped back into the house. She swiped her finger across the screen, unlocking it to reveal six missed calls and four unread text messages from her sister, Teresa.

She nearly dropped her phone on the kitchen floor when she read the most recent text.

Following mom's ambulance to Mount Sinai.

It's her heart. Get here fast!

Marie stood frozen in place, gasping for air. She'd lost her father years ago to a massive heart attack. Memories of the pain from that day flooded her mind. "Sam, get your shoes. We're leaving now."

Merciless tendrils of fear worked their way into the back of her mind, taking root to taint her every thought with torment. She'd already lost one person she loved today—she couldn't lose another. Not her mother.

Seventeen

Raul sat motionless, hunched over with his elbows resting on his knees. The beautiful scenery on the other side of the floor to ceiling windows of his Long Island beachfront home had no effect on his mood. There weren't enough waves in the ocean to wash away the pain he felt about what had happened between him and Marie the morning before.

What *had* happened? He'd gone over, bursting with excitement about getting their relationship back on track, and had left a single man. He scrubbed his hands over his face as if trying to erase the confusion clouding his mind. He let his arms drop back into place, resting on his legs, their heaviness rounding his broad shoulders.

Maybe Jonas had been right. He should have taken more time to deal with his problems before rushing off to see Marie. He'd wasted so much time alternating between either having his head in the sand or in the clouds. Trying to convince himself that Marie wasn't serious about fostering hadn't done him any favors.

He eyed a small box wrapped in brown shipping paper

sitting on the coffee table in front of him. His father's handwriting was as clear as the day he'd addressed the package. Jonas had made good on his promise to have it delivered. It almost seemed like a pointless exercise now that things were over between him and Marie. But he'd given his word to Jonas, and he always kept his word. Besides, he'd kept his father waiting for long enough. It was time to see what was inside.

An eerie feeling settled in the pit of his stomach when he thought of tearing the paper to reveal the contents of the box. After ten years, his father's last message to him had almost taken on a personality of its own.

Raul bit his bottom lip, prickles of both excitement and anxiety bouncing around in his stomach as he picked up the box. He ran his finger along a neatly folded crease on the side, the yellowed tape breaking free with little effort on his part. Unfolding the flap covering the end of the package, he was careful not to tear the aged paper. A small quiver in his hand halted his progress as he balled it into a fist, forcing his nerves into submission.

"I haven't been ignoring you, Dad." Raul's breathy words dissipated into the empty room around him. He released a long sigh laced with a decade of guilt and regret. "I just wasn't ready to say goodbye."

Armand walked into the room as Raul turned the package over to release the tape on the other side. The silver, domed plate cover on Armand's tray glinted in the sunlight filtering in through the windows. The thought of eating turned Raul's stomach sour.

He set the box on the table, relieved for any excuse to put off opening it up a little bit longer.

"I told you I'm not hungry, Armand. Just take it back to the kitchen. Please."

Armand marched up to where Raul sat and placed the tray of food on the coffee table, the metal tray clinking on the clear glass surface. "Monsieur, you have been home for more than a day, and still you have not eaten. If you are not sick, you must eat." Armand removed the platter cover to reveal an assortment of crackers and mild cheeses.

Pity softened his expression. "Please, Monsieur, allow me to leave this here for you."

Raul nodded and mumbled his gratitude as Armand retreated back into his domain.

Armand had been right. Raul hadn't eaten since before leaving Miami, and even then it hadn't been a full meal. He'd lost his appetite the day Marie suggested that they not see each other until the filming of his show was complete. How could he be expected to fill his gullet when everything that mattered in his life was broken?

Poking around at the crackers, he chose a plain wheat variety. He nibbled at the corner before tossing it back onto the plate and walking over to gaze out the window. Stretching his stiff limbs brought a little relief to his achy body. He'd barely slept in the last forty-eight hours, and he was beginning to feel the effects. He pressed the heel of his hand into his chest, rubbing it back and forth to ease the pain in his heart.

His stomach jolted when his phone sounded off from the next room. He hoped against hope that it was Marie. He had no idea what he could say or do that could fix things between them, but he needed to hear the sound of her voice. Rushing to the console table in the game room, he snatched the phone up.

His heart fell when he saw the name displayed on the screen. Why on earth would Kelsey St. James be calling him? She was Marie's best friend and fiancée to Mitch, one of his other old college buddies. He hadn't spoken to her for months.

Raul hesitated for a moment before answering. He really didn't feel like talking to anyone except Marie. But knowing that Kelsey and Mitch were still working in Kenya, he decided to answer—just in case they needed help of some kind.

"Kelsey? What's up?"

"I heard the news, Raul. Marie sent me a text yesterday, but she hasn't returned any of my texts or calls ever since. What's going on?" Kelsey's concern was evident in her strained tone.

Raul released a heavy sigh. He really didn't feel like getting into everything over the phone with his ex-girlfriend's best friend—a woman he barely knew. "It's complicated. We're on two different tracks in life. I guess we were doomed from the beginning. We just didn't know it yet."

An extra beat of silence followed Raul's confession.

"What are you talking about?" Kelsey asked. "Is Marie still at the hospital, or did she go home last night?"

Raul's knees buckled, causing him to stumble forward and catch himself on the nearest piece of furniture. "Marie's at the hospital? Which one? What happened?"

"You haven't heard? I would have thought you'd be the first one she'd call."

"I should have been, but I wasn't there for her yesterday. It's a long story, too long to go into right now. Is Marie okay?"

"She's fine. It's her mother. All I got yesterday was a text saying that her mom had a heart attack and they were considering emergency surgery at Mount Sinai. That was it! No updates. No returned calls. I'm worried about her, Raul. Can you go check on her?"

Raul's long strides brought him to the front door in a flash. "I'm on my way to the hospital now. Text you later."

He ended the call and speed-dialed Marie as he slipped into his vehicle. The tension in his shoulders mounted when his call went directly to voicemail. Throwing his car into reverse, he peeled out of the driveway, leaving his father's package lying unopened on the coffee table.

He was a man on a mission. Marie might not have been destined to be his bride, but that didn't change the fact that he was desperately in love with her. Even if they had no future together as a couple, he wasn't about to let her face this crisis alone.

EIGHTEEN

Marie sat at the end of a long padded hospital bench, her elbow resting on its narrow wooden arm. Sam was sprawled out beside her with his head lying in her lap. The day before had been long, and the night that followed had felt even longer.

Her eyes burned from lack of sleep. She could only imagine what shade of red they must be by now. Pressing her chin into her chest, she rolled her head from side to side, trying to work the kinks out. Of all the things she disliked about hospitals, she hated the waiting most of all.

She turned her eyes to the large monitor on the wall. Still no update on her mother's progress. Her pulse picked up its tempo. Surgery seemed to be taking longer than the doctor had anticipated. Taking a deep breath, she forced her nerves to settle. She couldn't allow herself to dwell on all of the possible scenarios continually playing over in her mind, vying for her attention. All she could do was sit and wait.

A chill wracked her body as her eyes traveled around the large waiting room. Never before had she felt so alone in a room full of people. Families huddled together in various nooks, chatting quietly, some happier than others. Nurses gathered behind tall desks, sharing quiet jokes and small talk. Marie had no one to confide in.

She'd sent Teresa home hours ago to get a few hours of sleep with her children, promising to call her if anything happened. Tony was seated across from her, but he offered little comfort. He slept with his head leaned back against the wall and his mouth hanging open. If the circumstances hadn't been so somber, she'd have been sure to snap plenty of photos to document the drool that trailed down his chin.

Marie ran a hand over Sam's buzz cut. A tired smile tugged at the corners of her mouth as she gazed down at his strawberry-blond hair. Teresa had offered to take him home with her to get away from the hospital for a few hours, but he'd refused.

"I can't leave Marie alone," he'd said.

Her eyes welled up at the memory. No amount of coaxing on her part would convince him to leave her side. As broken as her heart still was over losing Raul the day before, it was comforting to remember that she wasn't completely alone in the world. Oh, but what she wouldn't give right now for one last chance to fall into Raul's arms and feel her heartache fall away.

She heard a soft clearing of a throat behind her. Her heart leaped when she turned to see Raul standing only a few paces away with a cup of coffee in his hand. Steam escaped through the tiny hole in the lid as its fragrance filled her senses.

"I thought you might not have had your morning coffee yet." He offered an apologetic smile, holding the tall cup out to her.

Marie slipped out from under Sam's head. His bleary eyelids fluttered. She patted his cheek. "Rest here with

Tony, sweetheart. I'm going to walk down the hall a bit and talk to Raul for a few minutes. I'll be back." The boy nodded through a groggy fog and closed his eyes.

She motioned for Raul to walk with her down the wide corridor to a quiet place where they could talk. Every part of her being wanted to throw herself into his arms, but after the way they'd left things yesterday, she didn't feel quite right about it. "How did you know I was here?"

"Kelsey called this morning. She's been worried sick about you ever since you stopped answering your phone."

"What? I haven't—" Marie pulled her phone out of the shoulder bag hanging diagonally across her chest. She swiped her finger across the screen with no effect. "It's dead. I have no idea when it died. I hope Teresa hasn't been trying to call."

Raul handed her the coffee. "How's your mom?"

She held the cup with two hands, allowing the warmth from the liquid inside to seep into her cold fingers. Not daring to look into Raul's eyes, she stared at the white lid of her cup. "They confirmed it was a heart attack late last night. It wasn't nearly as bad as dad's was, but I don't think there's such a thing as a good heart attack. She's in surgery now. They're putting two stents in, but it's taking longer than they said it would."

Her breath caught in her throat when Raul took a step closer to her.

"How are you holding up?"

The kindness in his voice brought fresh tears to her eyes. She lifted her gaze only to find Raul studying her features. She struggled to keep her chin from quivering. "Just taking it one minute at a time." The next moment she found herself enveloped in Raul's warm embrace.

He whispered softly into her ear, "I'm so sorry I wasn't

here for you. Nothing about yesterday was right. I want to tell you everything I couldn't say then, but now isn't the time. Right now isn't about me, it's about you and your mother."

"If you're ready to talk, I'm ready to listen. Honestly, I'd love the chance to think about something else for a little while."

"Are you sure?"

Marie pulled away just enough to look him in the eyes. "I've never cared about anyone as much as I care about you. If you're ready to tell me what's been bothering you, I want to hear it."

Raul ran his hand down the length of her arm until he reached her hand. Giving it a gentle squeeze, he took a deep breath. "I realized a long time ago that I'll never be able to be a father—ten years ago, to be exact. I had the world's most amazing dad, Marie. You would have loved him. We did everything together. I always imagined myself growing up and becoming the same kind of father he was one day."

Marie listened quietly as his pained stare looked beyond her, and into a past filled with sorrow. The usual spark in his eyes was nowhere to be found. It had been replaced by weariness.

She caressed the back of his hand with the pad of her thumb. "What changed that dream?"

"One day he was gone. Dead." His eyes snapped back to hers. "I killed him." He passed a hand over his face, the crushing weight of his words turning the corners of his mouth downward.

"What? No, your father died in a plane crash. You showed me the article from the newspaper yourself."

"Where do you think he got the money to buy the plane? I gave it to him. It was one of the first things I did after we sold the company. I had a few billion dollars burning a hole in my pocket so I started throwing money around like a fool. I didn't give any thought to what the consequences might be."

Raul raked his fingers through his hair. "Dad had dreamed of flying since he was a kid. As soon as I had the money to make it happen, I did it! Sent him a check that would more than cover the cost of the type of plane he'd been eyeing for years—an ultralight."

Marie placed her hand over Raul's heart. "You were being a good son."

"No, a good son wouldn't give his father the means to kill himself. I'm responsible, Marie. If I hadn't given him that money, he'd be alive to this day. I'm guilty."

"The only thing you're guilty of is having a generous heart and loving your father. Grief is a powerful emotion. It's twisted the way you see your role in all of this. You didn't do anything wrong. You couldn't possibly have known what was going to happen."

"You're right. I didn't know what would happen if I bought him a plane, so I never should have done it. Actions have consequences, and I never gave them a second thought until it was too late."

Marie gazed up at him, wanting to speak but not knowing what to say.

"Don't you see? I'm too impulsive to be a father. I'd never be able to do the same things with my kids as my father did with me. Every time I'd try, I'd be brought back to another memory of me and Dad."

"But isn't that a good thing? Memories of our loved ones should be cherished, not boxed up and stuffed into some forgotten corner of our minds. It's hard at first, but over time—"

"It's been ten years. My feelings are just as raw today as they were years ago. I don't know if that will ever change. Now can you see why being a father isn't going to work for me?"

Marie closed her eyes and nodded. Raul had carried such a heavy weight for so many years. Even though he was all wrong, the guilt he felt was very real to him. It broke her heart to think of what the years since his father's passing must have been like for him.

"You're doing a great thing for Sam. He needs you, and you're going to be the most fantastic mother in history. I wish I could be a part of it, but—"

"Miss Maranzano?" The surgeon had walked up while they were engrossed in their conversation.

Marie latched onto Raul's arm.

"Your mother is out of surgery now."

Marie bit down on the inside of her cheek, anticipating the rest of the doctor's report.

"We had a bit of difficulty with some bleeding, but she pulled through and is resting well in the recovery room. We can allow one of you to sit with her while she continues to regain consciousness. I'll look in on her later this afternoon. I'll know better how long we'll need to keep her here at that time. If everything checks out, she may be able to go home this time tomorrow. For now, I'd say she's in pretty good shape."

Marie squeezed Raul's hand. "Thank you, Doctor."

She threw her arms around Raul's neck as the doctor walked away, sloshing her coffee in the process. Raul winced as hot coffee trickled down his back.

Releasing her hold on his neck, Marie grimaced. "I'm so sorry."

He chuckled. "It's okay. I'm just glad your mom's going to be all right."

Quiet settled between them. Marie tucked her hair behind her ear, unsure of where to fix her gaze.

Raul cleared his throat. "I guess you'd better get back to your mom."

She shook her head. "I've got Sam with me. They won't let him back there. I'll just wake Tony up. He can sit with her."

"Marie, you need to be there."

She looked up into his face, the compassion she found there made her heart flutter.

"Why don't you let me take Sam back to my place, so you can sit with her? I think it would mean a lot to your mom to have you there when she wakes up. I can keep Sam for as long as you need."

"That would be amazing. He's been such a good sport. We've been here since this time yesterday morning. Are you sure though? After everything you just told me—I just don't want things to be hard on you."

"I'll be fine. Your mom needs you. Besides, a hospital is no place for a kid."

Marie's face twisted with disappointment. "I just remembered—he can't go with you. You haven't done the paperwork to be cleared to care for a foster child. If I could be sure it would only be a couple of hours, it wouldn't be any big deal. But things can change so quickly in situations like these. I have no idea when I'd be able to get away to come and get him."

Raul held his phone up and wiggled it in the air. "Have you forgotten that I have a legion of hot-shot lawyers at my beck and call? Give me five minutes and I'll be cleared to babysit for the President of the United States."

She stepped in for another hug, this time easing her arms around his waist. She rested her head against his chest, every bit of tension melting away from her body. "Thank you so much."

"I'm glad I can do something to help. It's what friends are for." he said.

Marie sucked in a sharp breath, cringing at his words. A new knot formed in her stomach as they walked side-by-side, back to the waiting room. She wanted to take his hand and interlace her fingers with his, but that's not what friends did. Friends. This was her new normal. The man she loved with all of her heart was now, no more than a friend.

Nineteen

An afternoon that Raul had expected to feel awkward at best, had turned out to be some of the most fun he'd had in a while. There was something special about spending time with someone who was unimpressed by his wealth. To Sam, Raul was just a cool dude with cool toys. It was a nice change of pace from the usual schmoozing crowd that always tried to worm their way into his good graces.

Marie had been able to convince Sam to leave the hospital after he found out that her mother was out of surgery. Once he knew Marie could be with her instead of left alone in the waiting room, he was willing to go. He was a loyal kid. It was easy to see why Marie had fallen in love with him so quickly.

Now, they sat side by side at Raul's beach front home, their plush leather seats rumbling in time with the video game they played. The big screen lit up Raul's darkened media room enough for him to see Sam's wide grin as he clutched the controller in his hand. They raced their cars around a mock-up of a Formula One track Raul had driven several times in person.

Video games hadn't been this much fun since his college days. Easing back on the accelerator, he let his car drift off the track just enough to allow Sam to pass. After everything life had dealt the poor kid, Raul figured it was about time for him to get a few wins under his belt. Sam's iridescent-purple car whizzed past Raul's, crossing the finish line just ahead of him.

"Man, you're good," Raul said. "Maybe I should hire you to drive for me in Monaco next season. What do you think? Would Marie let you out of school to go win a few races for me?"

Sam's laughter was brief, his smile replaced by a pensive look. "Who knows where I'll be next year. They never let you stay anywhere long when you're a foster kid."

"You've been in other foster homes before?"

Sam scrolled through the vehicles in the virtual garage on the television screen. "Yeah, any time my mom got into trouble I'd get sent somewhere new."

The matter-of-fact way Sam talked about his upbringing tugged on Raul's heart. "You're a really strong young man, you know that?"

Sam puckered his lips and scrunched his freckled nose. "That's what they all say."

"You don't sound very convinced." Raul craned his neck to catch a glimpse of the boy's eyes and recognized something familiar in them. It was very much like looking into a mirror. Sam wore the same mask of bravery Raul had constructed for himself over the years. But he knew what lay behind masks and it wasn't something any nine-year-old little boy should have to deal with.

Sam selected his car and busied himself tricking it out with every upgrade available.

Raul got up to stretch his legs and wandered to the other side of the room. "Does it bother you when people say you're strong?"

"Yeah, they don't know me. They're just glad I don't cry myself to sleep 'cause they don't want to hear it. Just because you don't cry out loud, doesn't mean you're strong though."

Sam's powerful words pierced Raul's heart. He wondered how many times the child he was looking at had cried himself to sleep silently with no one to dry his tears or comfort his hurting heart. "What *does* it mean when you don't cry out loud?"

The boy shrugged. "It means you're alone."

Alone. Raul had spent the majority of the past ten years of his life alone, living life behind a mask. That was no life for a child.

Now things were starting to make sense. Sam had stuck with Marie overnight at the hospital because he was trying to protect her from feeling alone, too. He was a good kid—too good to spend the rest of his childhood bouncing around in the system, waiting for an adoptive family that may never materialize. Marie was right to take him in and make him her own.

"I spent a lot of time being alone, too," Raul said. "Then I met Marie and everything changed." His chest constricted when Sam gazed up at him, the brokenness of his young heart evident in his pained expression.

"That's the way it was for me, too. But it won't last." Tears welled up in Sam's green eyes.

Before Raul had a chance to second guess himself, he was across the room, draping his arm around Sam's shoulders. "Just because you've been alone in the past doesn't mean you have to be alone in the future. I happen to know for a fact that everything is going to turn out all right for you. Do you trust me?"

Sam hesitated, studying Raul's face for a long moment. "It's not usually a good idea."

"What's not?" asked Raul.

"Trusting someone."

Looking into the eyes of an innocent child as he quietly pleaded for help drove every fear from Raul's heart. "Take a chance on me."

For the first time in years, Raul wasn't afraid. He wasn't afraid to feel. He wasn't afraid to remember. There were more important things to consider. A wounded child stood in front of him. Sam was a boy who needed love—who needed a father. Raul filled his lungs to capacity, gleaning strength from the very boy who needed him the most.

Raul's heart flooded with raw emotions when his own father's words rose up from deep inside, replaying in his mind with as much clarity as the day they'd been spoken. *"A real man doesn't do what's best for himself; he does what's best for those he loves."*

It was as if a bolt of light straight out of heaven shot down on him, illuminating everything about his life in that moment. He'd been lost in a dark place for so long that he'd accepted the lie that there was no way out. But this was it. Love. Pure, unselfish love was the only way to find his way toward peace and leave the torment of the last decade behind.

Life was never meant to be lived nursing wounds and hiding away from people who needed you. He could see that now. A sudden rush of excitement filled his body, energizing him like he'd never known before. It was time to stop worrying about himself and become the man his father had raised him to be.

Anticipation stirred in the pit of his stomach at the thought of opening his father's package. It still lay on the coffee table where he'd left it earlier that morning, partially opened. He gave Sam's shoulders a quick squeeze. "I've got to go take care of something real quick. You can keep playing here if you want. I'll be back."

Only a few hours before, it had taken every ounce of his strength to force himself to even consider opening the package. But things had changed since then. It was time to see what was inside. He was ready to stop hiding.

Raul squinted at the sunlight streaming into the back room of the house as his eyes adjusted from the darkened room he'd just left. Sitting in the same seat as before, he took the box in his hands. He released the tape from the underside and pulled the brown shipping paper away. Inside the brown cardboard box, he found a smaller box rolled in bubble wrap, with an envelope lying on top.

He pulled the yellowed paper from the envelope and gazed at his father's handwriting. Taking a deep steadying breath, he read his father's last words to him.

Son,

I've been trying to get a hold of you all week to thank you for your gift. I was so proud when your check came in the mail. Not because you're now a very wealthy man, but because one of your first acts after making your fortune was to reach out and do something for someone else. You're a good man, son. Never change.

I never told you or your mother, but I've been tucking away money here and there whenever I could to get that ultralight one day. It took a lot of years, but I finally saved up enough to get one. I knew you wouldn't mind, so I went ahead and spent the money you sent on your mother. It isn't every day a man gets his hands on that kind of money, and I wanted to do something special for her instead of buying a nicer aircraft for myself.

Our anniversary isn't for another two months, so I'm sending her gift to you for safe-keeping. You know your mother—she always finds every present I try to hide from her. I want this one to be a surprise! I figure you can keep it in the fancy safe your building has. This is going to knock her socks off. She thinks I bought the ultralight with the money you sent. I can't wait to see her face when she sees what I actually spent it on.

Raul rested the hand holding the letter on his knee as he used his other to clear his eyes of the tears blurring his vision. The letter fell from his shaky hands before he finished reading it. He fumbled with the bubble wrap still wound around the box, pulling it off to reveal a flat, square box. It was bright red with the word *Cartier* engraved in golden letters on the top.

He set it on the table and scrambled to his knees in front of it. Running his fingertips across the surface, his mind raced to process the thoughts swirling there. He placed his elbows on either side of the jewelry box, and grabbed handfuls of hair from the crown of his head. The room spun around him as the thundering pounding of his heartbeat boomed in his ears. The truth of what had actually happened all those years ago was like a key, unlocking the chains shackling him to the past.

He reached down, and opened the hinged lid revealing a platinum necklace with a single pendant hanging from it. The teardrop-shaped ruby dazzled his eyes as it refracted the afternoon sun. Taking the pendant in his fingers, he ran the pad of his thumb over the heart-cut diamond nestled into the platinum setting just above the ruby. It was just his mother's style; delicate and feminine.

Raul squeezed his eyes shut, trying to hold the tears back. His father's scrawled handwriting lit up his mind's eye like an LED billboard. *I spent the money you sent on your mother.* Raul hadn't had a hand in his father's death.

His shoulders shook as voiceless sobs poured out of him, the hot tears streaking his face washing away years of needless guilt. His father's death, though a tragic accident, hadn't been his fault.

A small, warm hand came to rest on Raul's back. "You can cry out loud. I don't mind." Sam patted his shoulder with a tenderness that melted Raul's heart.

It was as if he'd been reborn. He turned to look Sam in the eyes. With tears still streaming down his face, a fierce love for the boy he gazed at bloomed in his heart. He cupped the boy's round cheek in his hand. "Sam, we're both going to be okay. We're all done being alone."

In only a moment's time, Raul had a clear vision of the future. He knew what he wanted, he knew what Marie wanted, and for the first time in a long while, it was the same thing. Not many people got a chance to get a do-over, but Raul was going to make it happen. It was time to go back to the beginning and do things right from the start.

The doorbell sounded, pulling Raul back into the present. He stood and dried his tears before heading to the front door. It was Marie's sister, Teresa. He opened it, heart bursting with excitement. If he was going to pull off his plan, he'd need help, and Teresa was just the person for the job.

"Hey Raul, I'm here to pick up Sam."

Raul peered around Teresa, checking the car to see if Marie had come along.

"They're releasing mom tomorrow. Marie is at home getting her house ready for Mom to come and stay with her for a little while. She thought it might be easier for the two of you if I stopped by for Sam, you know?"

The look of pity in her eyes didn't faze him. "Come in, Teresa! You're exactly who I needed to see. I need your help." Raul was a man on a mission, and it was time to enlist the troops it would take to get the job done.

He'd faltered and nearly failed to protect Marie's heart, but never again. She needed a man to cherish her. Sam needed a father to stand by him. Raul would be that man for both of them.

Twenty

Marie stood at the kitchen table, sorting through three days worth of mail that had piled up since her mother had been released from the hospital. Having a recovering house guest underfoot gave her plenty to do, but no amount of busyness could distract her from the gaping hole in her heart. She'd lost the only man she'd ever really loved, and there wasn't anything she could do about it.

"Two ships passing in the night." She felt like the living embodiment of the old cliché. Though their time together had made an indelible mark on her life, there was no question about it—her and Raul's lives were set on two different courses that would likely never intersect again.

A familiar lump formed in Marie's throat as she recalled their last meeting for the hundredth time that day. She couldn't fix what was broken between them. As long as Raul carried that crushing weight of guilt on his shoulders, he'd always shy away from the family life that Marie dreamed of.

"Marie, didn't I teach you to make coffee better than

this?" Marie's mother walked into the room carrying a barely touched cup of black coffee, steam rising from its surface.

"It's decaf, Ma."

"No wonder I'm dying over here. Where are you hiding the good stuff?"

"No, Ma. You know caffeine makes your heart race. No regular coffee." Marie handed her mother the stack of cards she'd just pulled from the pile of junk mail. "It looks like a lot of people want you to get well soon. Let's try not to disappoint them." She flashed her mother a wry smile.

The older, but no less feisty woman poured the contents of her mug down the kitchen sink. "Is that the doctor's orders, or just my know-it-all first-born's?"

"It's my orders," Marie said. She gazed at her mother's back as she stood at the sink with steam rising up from the coffee running down the drain. Marie's heart constricted when she thought of how close she'd come to losing her the other day. Squeezing her eyes shut, she shook her head to clear her mind. Mama was going to be okay. Marie would see to that.

"All right. All right." Her mother walked over and cupped her cheeks with her soft hands. She tilted Marie's head, pulling it down to plant a kiss in the middle of her forehead. "For you, I'll give up caffeine—but not chocolate. I'll die before I give up chocolate."

Marie laughed. "You've got yourself a deal."

Teresa's twin boys burst into the house through the side door and raced into the kitchen ahead of their mother. "Hi, Aunt Marie. Bye, Aunt Marie." Their little voices spoke in unison as they clattered through the room and up the stairs.

"What? No love for your grandmother?" Marie's

mother called after them with a loud voice, arms outstretched.

"All they're thinking about is playing with Sam. Don't take it personal, Ma. Why don't you open a few of those cards? I'm sure you'll start feeling the love once you read a few of them." She offered her mother a warm smile, but no matter how many times she put a smile on her lips, the joy never reached her heart. Inside, she was miserable.

A moment later Teresa hurried in after the boys, carrying a load of groceries. Plopping them on the counter, she gave her mother a questioning look. "Sorry I'm late. Did I miss anything?"

"What are you talking about, Teresa?" Marie said. "I'm on leave. We're not on any kind of schedule. There's nothing to miss." She shook her head and chuckled in spite of herself at her sister's intensity.

"This one isn't mine." Marie's mother held up one of the cards for her daughter to see. "It's addressed to you. My friends all know that I don't answer to Marie. They call me Maria or they get ignored."

Marie took the card and inspected it, turning it over in her hands.

"Who's it from?" Teresa said, wagging her eyebrows.

Marie rolled her eyes at her sister's sing-song voice. "Cut it out with the whole raised eyebrows thing, Teresa. There isn't anything special about this card."

"I wouldn't be so sure of that if I were you," Teresa said. "Open it!"

Marie's brows drew together as she read the note written on the inside of the card. Her usual soft features morphed into a steely expression with lips pressed into a hard, thin line.

"Well?" Teresa could barely contain her enthusiasm.

"Remember that movie maker I was helping? It turns out he's not a movie maker after all. It was all a set-up to get pictures and sound bites of me for that awful TV producer. I always thought there was something fishy about Miles, but I couldn't put my finger on it. He was secretly recording me whenever we met up."

"What? I'm confused." Teresa snatched the card from Marie's hands and read it for herself. "This doesn't make any sense."

"I suppose he's got a conscience, after all. Look"—Marie pointed to the second to last paragraph—"He says right here that once Raul's show got canceled, he and Meg were out of work. Now, she's been pressuring him to give her everything he had on me. Apparently she wants to plaster my face all over her Internet tabloid, but he's not going to give her the goods. He sent the note to apologize for everything."

"Not, that." Teresa waved the card in the air. "This card wasn't supposed to be from some out-of-work TV guy."

"Who did you think it was going to be from?" Marie asked. She knew the answer to that question. Teresa had been acting odd ever since she'd picked Sam up from Raul's place. Having her sister face Raul that day was supposed to have been the easy way out, but she was beginning to regret bringing Teresa into the mix.

"Well..." Teresa shrugged, struggling to find the right words to say.

"Raul? Did you expect it to be from him? Teresa, you've got to stop it with this. Raul and I are done." The words cut into Marie's heart when she said them, but she couldn't live with the false hope that Teresa seemed to be holding on to.

"Nothing is ever done, Marie. Not unless you want it to be," Teresa said.

All Marie could do was roll her eyes. Her sister would never understand. She and Raul wanted completely different things out of life—dreams that couldn't possibly coexist. Of course she didn't want things to be over, but they were.

At that moment, three sets of feet thundered down the wooden stairs, and tromped to the picture window in the living room overlooking the front yard. "Whoa, I've never seen one that big before," said one of the boys.

Relieved for an excuse to change the subject, Marie headed to the living room to see what the commotion was all about, her mother and sister following along. A knock sounded at the front door before she reached the picture window where the boys still stood, staring at something outside.

Marie looked through the peephole and saw an unfamiliar man dressed in a black suit jacket and tuxedo pants. He stood at attention on her front porch. Looking past him, she spied the longest stretch limo she'd ever seen, parked on the road in front of her house.

Teresa shoved her out of the way and snuck a peek. She stepped back with a satisfied grin plastered on her face. She crossed her arms across her chest. "Well, are you going to open the door, or are you going to let the man petrify on the front porch?" she said.

Marie only knew one person who would arrive at her home in a limo. Raul. Her stomach leapt at the thought of his name while twisting into knots at the same time. Her heart wanted to see him more than anything in the world, but her head knew she needed to close that door and lock it up tight. She couldn't keep seeing a man she was wildly in love with if they had no future together. It would be torture.

Marie's mother reached for the doorknob and threw the door wide open. "Come on in."

The man in black stepped into the house, holding a single pink carnation in one hand and a small golden envelope in the other. "I'm looking for Miss Maranzano?"

Teresa pushed Marie forward.

"That would be me." Marie took the flower and envelope, acutely aware of her family's eyes watching her every move. She pulled a piece of monogrammed stationary out of the envelope and read Raul's simple message.

I want to go back to where everything went wrong, and make it right. Give me one more chance. I promise I won't disappoint you. Come and meet me—I'm waiting for you!

Marie's hands trembled at the words she'd just read. Dared she hope that they still had a chance? Sure, he promised that he wouldn't disappoint her, but she wasn't convinced he knew how important being a mother—being Sam's mother—was to her. Raul's heart was in the right place, she had no doubt about that. Of course he didn't want to hurt her, but she'd thought they were on the same page before, and that was when things had gone terribly wrong.

Teresa's hot breath tickled Marie's neck as her sister read the note over her shoulder. "Well, what do you say, Marie?"

Marie's mother took the note and gave it a quick read. "Of course she's going to go. Marie, you're going to go, right?"

"I don't know, Ma." Marie glanced at Sam who now stood only a few feet away. "Things are complicated."

"The man said he won't disappoint," Teresa said. "You

love him, Marie. Give him a chance. You two were made for each other."

Marie hesitated. Her heart pulled her in one direction while her head pulled her in the opposite one. Raul had seemed so certain about everything he'd said only a few days before. But if there was even the tiniest of chances that they could work things out, she couldn't walk away.

Convinced that her family could survive one evening without her, she took a deep breath and nodded. "All right, I'll go." A shiver of anticipation raced down her spine at her own words.

Teresa let out a cry of excitement as she opened the hall closet and pulled out two large suitcases.

"What are those for?" Marie asked.

"They're for you," Teresa said. "Raul may or may not have asked for my help with his grand plan to get you back."

"I'm just going to talk to him. We're not eloping. How long do you expect this conversation to last?"

"A couple of days at least. It takes a while to get to Japan." Teresa winked at her older sister.

"Japan? I can't go to Japan! I can't leave Mom for that long."

"I'm fine, Marie. I've still got Teresa and Tony to look after me." She laid both hands on Marie's shoulders and looked her in the eyes. "You were worried about what caffeine might do to my heart, right? What do you think it would do to my heart if I knew you turned down a chance at something beautiful with that boy because of me?"

Marie didn't have an answer. "But Sam. I can't leave him for days on end."

Sam slipped up to Marie and took her hand. "Don't worry about me, Marie. I was at Raul's house for a long time—I know things. I think he needs you as much as I do. I could tell. You should go see him."

"Honey, that's so sweet of you to say, but legally, I can't just leave you behind at the drop of a hat."

Teresa fished a piece of paper out of her purse and waved it in front of Marie's face. "Sam can stay with me. I'm certified by the State of New York."

"How is that even possible? Certification can take months." Marie's mouth hung open.

Teresa laughed as she folded the paper and stashed it away in her purse again. "You know what they say. Money talks. And Raul's money can talk for days! A few phone calls from his lawyers, and the application I put in more than two months ago was expedited and pushed through the system."

Sam's green eyes peered into Marie's. "You should go. You're happier when you're his friend."

Sam wasn't wrong. She was definitely happier with Raul in her life. He made her happier than she'd ever known was possible.

He cupped his hand over his mouth to whisper into Marie's ear. "I think he wants to marry you."

The warmth in her heart rushed up her neck, causing her ears to burn. Marie wrapped Sam in a hug as tears threatened to spill onto her flushed cheeks.

Three main desires had followed Marie throughout her childhood and into adult life. For as long as she could remember, she'd always told people that she wanted to be a teacher, get married, and be a mom when she grew up. This was her last chance to see if her dream would ever become a reality. If she couldn't enjoy married life with Raul, she didn't want it with anyone.

"Okay, I'll go."

The driver took the suitcases. "If you'll follow me, Miss Maranzano. Mr. De Luca's jet is prepped and waiting for you."

Marie took one final look over her shoulder at her family as she walked toward the limousine. Five bright faces crowding the doorway smiled back at her as she offered one final wave before setting off on a journey that would take her to the other side of the world.

She climbed into the darkened interior of the limo and settled into her soft leather seat. The outside world dropped away when the driver shut the door. Marie swallowed hard and buried her face in her hands. She hoped she wasn't making a mistake. Her heart had shattered the first time they'd parted ways. If they weren't able to make things right between them this time, it might never recover.

Twenty-One

Marie clutched at her wooden bench seat and took a deep breath, savoring the briny smell of the sea around her. It felt good to breathe the fresh air again after spending hours cooped up in Raul's jet. The flight over had been more than comfortable in her luxurious surroundings, but the opulence of the private aircraft paled in comparison to the raw natural beauty of the bay.

Overhead, lowering clouds heavy with rain blocked out the sunlight, bathing the world in gray. Ocean spray hit her in the face as the same small fishing boat took her to the island where she and Raul had celebrated their three month anniversary back in August. So much had changed in the two months that had passed since then. She'd gone from being convinced that Raul was her future, to losing him entirely.

Looking over her shoulder, she gazed at the familiar, wrinkled fisherman piloting the craft. With his hand on the wheel, he focused intently, eyes busy reading the choppy seas he navigated.

More questions than she could count flooded her mind, all competing for her attention. She'd tried to call Raul while they were refueling on the West coast, but hadn't been able to get through. All their troubles would be over if Raul had had a change of heart about having a family. She wanted to believe that he had, but she couldn't. Not yet. She had to guard her heart against getting carried away by the romance of being whisked off to a romantic rendezvous.

There was no way to know what Raul was thinking until they spoke. She was done assuming things where their relationship was concerned. The emotions filling her heart churned just as much as the rough seas tossing the boat.

The sound of the surf crashing on a rocky shoreline told her that they were almost there. Her secluded island destination loomed just ahead. She turned her attention to a horizon veiled in sheets of rain and bit her bottom lip, the taste of sea salt filling her mouth. What was she going to say when she saw Raul?

A sudden feeling of self-consciousness washed over her as she smoothed her hands over her clothing. She hadn't seen Raul since their last meeting at the hospital when she'd worn a two-day-old outfit wrinkled from her overnight stay. She wanted to look her best for him today, but Teresa had only packed her most boring clothes. Her wide-legged black gaucho pants and snug black sequin tank would have to do. She hugged a royal-blue cardigan around her torso to shut out some of the blustery October wind.

The old man pulled up alongside the dock and tethered the boat in place. Marie scanned the shoreline for Raul, but didn't see him anywhere. She took the fisherman's hand, and stepped onto the dock. From her new vantage point, she could see a large arrow drawn in the sand with a single pair of footprints leading down the beach and around a large stand of boulders.

Her shoulders shook with the massive shiver that raced down her spine as she followed in Raul's footsteps. The moment of truth had arrived. In only a matter of minutes she would learn, for better or for worse, what her future would look like.

RAUL STOOD ON THE SANDY BEACH WITH HIS EYES fixed on a large rocky outcropping. He'd spied Marie's boat approaching the dock a few minutes before. She'd round the corner any minute. He wiped perspiration from his brow and muttered the speech he'd prepared one final time.

He wet his lips and tugged at the hem of his shirt as a low rumble of thunder rolled in from somewhere far out to sea. But the storm brewing out there was nothing compared to the storm raging in the pit of his stomach.

He'd been so sure of himself while making his plans to sweep Marie off her feet, but now that it was showtime, he felt woefully unprepared. He glanced behind him at the solid wood pavilion at the other end of the beach. Its thick, redwood beams supported a multi-tiered tile roof that curved upward at each corner. Between each post stretched an intricate wooden lattice work from which bamboo and paper lanterns hung, swinging in the wind.

Had he done enough to make this moment special? Probably, but he wasn't sure about anything anymore. Marie wasn't the type to have her head turned by extravagance. Maybe he'd gone too far. He probably should have just gone over to her house and had a heart-to-heart on her porch swing. That was more her speed. Why had he—

Raul sucked in a sharp breath. There she was, standing in his footprints with a hand resting on the large boulder beside her. With a hammering heart, he watched as her hair whipped out behind her in the wind. Her sequin shirt clung to her in all the right places, sparkling even in the stormy-gray light of day. She looked every inch a goddess of the sea, risen to steal the hearts of men. Raul's Adam's apple bobbed as he tried in vain to swallow his nerves.

Mesmerized by her swaying hips as she trudged through the ever shifting sand, every one of his carefully planned words abandoned him. There he stood, with nothing but stammering lips and a heart overflowing with love to offer the single most gorgeous woman he'd ever laid eyes on.

Marie walked up to within a few feet of him before she stopped, an unreadable expression on her face. "Hi," she said, offering a guarded smile.

"Hi." Raul squeezed the back of his neck as if hoping to coax more words to pop out of his mouth. "I—uh, how was your flight?" If it wouldn't have made him look like a crazy man, he would have punched himself in the side of the head for such a stupid opening line. Why hadn't he said something profound, or romantic even? He needed his brain to start functioning—stat.

"It was nice." Marie caught a handful of hair, twisted it, and pulled it over the front of her shoulder, trying to contain it in the rising wind.

Lightning arced between the clouds above the water only a few miles away. It was as if the charged air shocked Raul back to life. He stepped toward Marie. It took every ounce of his will power to keep his hands off her. "Marie," he said, voice husky with emotion. "I asked you to come here because I wanted to go back to the place where things went wrong. Nothing but you, me, and the sea."

"I like that." She looked up at him through her thick, dark lashes, causing his stomach to turn a flip.

He reached out and took her hand, interlacing his fingers with hers. "The last time we were here, you tried to share something very special with me. You tried to share a piece of your heart, and I didn't listen. I heard the words you said, but I didn't *listen*." He lifted her hand to his lips and placed a lingering kiss on her knuckles. "I was lost, Marie. So lost, you can't even imagine."

The look of unconditional love in Marie's eyes as she gazed up into his was nearly overpowering, and weakened his knees.

"You were hurting. I know that now," she said.

The thundering of his heart was so loud it blocked out the sound of the approaching storm. "I've changed. I'm not the same guy I was even a few days ago. I've grown up, Marie, and I did it for you. I did it because of you. It's always been about you. You're it for me."

He searched her eyes for a long moment. "Give me another chance. Let's go back in time to that night when we stood in this very spot. Tell me what you want out of life. What are your hopes? What are your dreams?"

Marie's chin quivered, teary eyes blinking, trying desperately to hold back the floodgates.

Raul leaned in close and whispered in her ear, the sweet scent of her hair making his head spin. "Trust me with your heart one more time. I'll protect it with everything I've got."

She pulled back just enough to look him in the eyes. "I've only ever wanted one thing, a family of my own to love." She shrugged off her trembling voice and offered a smile that didn't reach her eyes, stretching her trembling lips thin.

Raul closed the remaining gap between them and wrapped an arm around Marie's waist. With his broad hand spanning the small of her back, he gazed into her eyes. "That's exactly what I want, too."

He could have sworn that he was struck by a bolt of lightning when Marie laid her delicate hand on his chest. She stared at him with a mixture of hope and confusion swirling in her wide, brown eyes.

"But what about your dad—and kids? I thought you couldn't..."

Raul brushed a few wisps of hair out of her face with his free hand, and worked his fingers into the thick locks at the base of her neck. Cupping the back of her head with his hand, he drew her closer. He took a deep breath to steady his racing pulse, but it was no use. As long as Marie was this close, it was a lost cause. "I've made peace with the past. There's nothing holding me back now."

Tears streamed down Marie's cheeks. "Do you mean it?"

"Every word." Raul's heart sang when Marie leaned into him, her curves melding with the lean lines of his own body as the first raindrops began to fall.

Marie's hot breath teased his lips. "It's starting to rain." Her breathless voice invited him to make the next move.

"I don't care." He muttered the words, lost in the moment before pressing his lips against hers. How he'd missed the softness of her sweet lips. He kissed her with such passion, it was as if it were their first, last, and every kiss in between, all wrapped up into one. Marie slid her arms around his neck, giving as much as he gave, oblivious to the downpour around them. Desire lit a fire that coursed through his veins that no amount of rain could dampen as he deepened the kiss.

A crack of lightening in the sky above them broke their

trance. Raul pulled away, chest still heaving. "Come on." He nodded toward the pavilion. "I think you'll like what's next." He grabbed her hand, and they took off running down the beach toward the shelter the ancient structure had to offer.

Once inside, Marie wrung out her hair and peeled her sopping wet cardigan off, dropping it to the floor with a slap.

Raul raked his fingers through his hair, slinging it to the side and out of his face. He stretched his arms wide. "What do you think?"

"I think it's not fair that we just ran through the same rain storm, and you still look like a fashion model while I look like a drowned rat."

Raul dropped his chin to his chest, his shoulders shaking with laughter. "You could never look like a drowned rat." He stepped close and rested both hands on her hips. "You look like a siren of the sea, and I'm powerless to resist."

Marie held on tight as he placed a trail of kisses along her jaw line, stopping when he reached the corner of her mouth. Squeezing his eyes shut, he forced himself to step back and get himself together. If he looked at her full lips another minute, he knew he'd fall under their spell again and never finish what he'd set out to do this afternoon.

He cleared his throat. "I was actually referring to this place. What do you think of it?"

Colorful paper lanterns hung from the lattice work beneath the eves and swayed from the rafters above their heads. They glowed all the brighter as the storm outside grew darker. A small candlelit table was set for two at the other end of the pavilion, well away from the rain blowing in through the open walls.

"It's the most romantic thing I've ever seen," she said.

Raul's heart skipped a beat. "Is it really?"

Marie sighed in response as a dreamy smile lit up her face.

Raul had more conviction about the next words he was about to say than anything else he'd ever said in his life. "I was going to wait until later, but I think now is the time."

Without another word, he took Marie by the hand and dropped to one knee. "I don't want to waste another second of my life without you by my side. I love you. I want you to be my wife, and I want Sam to be our son. Will you marry me?"

Marie clapped a hand over her mouth, stifling her scream. Once the squeal had run its course, she fanned her face wildly with both hands as she struggled to catch her breath.

Raul inclined his head to catch her eye. "I'm hoping that means yes?"

"Quit talking and kiss me, you big hunky chunk of beefcake. Of course I'll marry you!" Marie flung herself at him and wrapped her arms around his neck. She pulled his face close to hers and smothered it with kisses, leaving trails of bright-red lipstick in her wake.

Raul dug into his pocket and produced a small box. "Let's make it official." He opened the hinged lid, revealing a solitaire diamond engagement ring. Its round brilliant cut reflected the lantern light above, glimmering in its bed of black velvet. Sliding it onto her finger was the final step on his long road to healing. He would never again be a lone wolf, racing to outrun his past. He'd spend the rest of his life being the man his father had raised him to be. The man Marie had always known he could be. The man he wanted to be.

Epilogue

The air smelled of cinnamon and nutmeg as Marie sat curled up on Raul's couch. She gazed out the window of his Long Island home, watching snowflakes illuminated by the sconces on either side of the back door as they flittered to the ground.

A thick blanket of snow lay on the deck overlooking the cold Atlantic, but the fire crackling nearby gave off a warm glow that reached all the way to her heart. The soft carols falling on her ears brought a smile to her face, reminding her of cherished memories from Christmases long past.

Sam sat on the floor, surrounded by torn wrapping paper and a mountain of gifts—the first he'd ever received for Christmas in his nine years of life. Long strands of ribbon reflected the white lights decorating a ten-foot tree dressed in red and gold. No more presents remained beneath it, but that didn't mean that the magic of Christmas Eve was over just yet.

Raul walked up behind Marie. Bending down to place a soft kiss on the top of her head, he gave her shoulders a light squeeze. "Are you ready?"

Butterflies danced in her stomach. They'd saved Sam's best gift for last, and she could hardly wait for him to open it. She placed her hand on Raul's and nodded. "I'm so ready."

Raul walked around the couch and over to where Sam sat. "It looks like there's one more present for you to open, buddy." He held out a rectangular box wrapped in red foil paper with a silver bow on top.

Sam's brows raised. "Another one?" He took the gift and played with the bow for a moment.

"Yep, this is it," Marie said. "This is the last one to open, but I think you'll be able to enjoy it for a long time."

Sam ran his hand over his present, but hesitated to open it.

"What are you waiting for? Open it!" Marie was giddy with excitement.

A pensive look washed over Sam's features. "I kind of don't want tonight to ever end."

"Neither do I, buddy," Raul said. "But try not to think of this present as the end of something fun, but as the beginning of something even better."

"Like what?" Sam asked.

"Just open it, sweetie," Marie said. "You'll see what we mean in a minute."

Sam tore into the paper like a pro and lifted the lid. Inside was a framed photo of the three of them from their first outing together. He touched the glass and smiled. "A picture of my first helicopter ride. That was one of the best days ever." He hugged the box to his chest.

"It sure was, and this picture is one of my all time favorites. I love it because my two best guys are in it," Marie said.

Raul cleared his throat. "Family pictures are really

important to Marie and me. We plan to take a lot more of them after our wedding this spring. But the thing is, we don't want to take a single family photo without you in it. What do you think about that?"

"I don't mind taking pictures that much," Sam said, oblivious to the meaning behind Raul's last words.

"Sweetheart, we're asking you to be a part of our forever family. We want to adopt you." Marie struggled in vain to keep her voice steady, its wavering tone revealing the depth of her emotions.

Sam clutched the box that still held the picture and buried his face, hiding it in the tissue paper. The only indication of Sam's reaction was the sound of his sniffling. Marie wanted to rush to his side and comfort him, but held back to allow Raul to have a moment with him.

Raul knelt beside Sam and laid his hand on the boy's back. The faintest of muffled sobs escaped Sam's lips, bringing a fresh wave of tears to Marie's eyes. She placed a hand over her mouth, and bit her bottom lip. She had to keep it together. If she started crying now, there would be no stopping it.

"You can cry out loud, Sam. You're not alone anymore," Raul said.

Sam leapt to his feet and threw his arms around Raul's neck, clinging to him as he cried openly. Raul wrapped the boy in his strong arms, the tenderness of his embrace melting Marie's heart.

Once his sobs subsided, Sam pulled back and spoke, tears still streaking his face. "You're going to be my dad?"

Raul fought back tears of his own, but lost his battle. "Yes." He choked the word out with a smile tugging at the corners of his lips.

"I've never had a dad before."

"Well, you've got one from now on," Raul said. "And a mom who loves you more than you can imagine."

Tears streamed down Marie's cheeks as she watched her heart's desire come true right before her eyes. She joined Raul and Sam on the floor and wrapped her arms around them, knowing that from that moment on, their three hearts were knitted together as one. They shared an unbreakable bond—a forever love.

The End

Become a VIP Today

Do you love sweet and swoony clean romance? If so, I'd like to invite you to join my VIP Readers Club mailing list!

I share weekly book updates, FANTASTIC deals, and exclusive news with my VIP readers! Plus you'll receive special sales, contests, and giveaways.

Join the club and become a VIP today to receive the FREE prequel novella for the Wounded Warrior Rescue series, *Mending His Heart,* as my gift to you!

Visit www.KristenIten.com to sign up!

What to Read Next...

He's a billionaire on a mission. She's on her way to Paris. Will their new business arrangement get in the way?

Jonas is on the verge of bankruptcy, but that's not what keeps him up at night. He can't let down his employees—not if he wants to keep the promise he made to his late mother. He has one chance to turn his business around, and it all depends on striking a deal with an eccentric billionaire in south Texas who's expecting a visit from him and his fiancée.

But there's just one problem...

Jonas's spoiled fiancée has no intention of taking part in anything so *pedestrian* as a business trip. But if Jonas can't show his potential new business partner that he's a stable family man, everyone who depends on his company will be put in jeopardy—including his administrative assistant, Lily.

When Lily walked into her boss's office with her resignation letter in hand, the last thing she expected was to leave the room ten minutes later with a new job description: *fake fiancée*. But she can't turn down the kind of money Jonas is offering for a single day on the job—not when it could fund her goal of moving to Paris and pursuing the career of her dreams.

But what happens when a quick job turns out to be a whole lot longer than they bargained for? Will their hearts survive the strain of faking emotions that have their root in reality?

Visit KristenIten.com to learn where you can purchase your copy of A Sincere Billionaire's Fake Fiancee today!

Have You Read the Wounded Warrior Rescue Series Yet?

Mending His Heart
eBook Available for FREE at KristenIten.com

Mending His Past
Mending His Dream
Mending His Scars
Mending His Trust
Mending His Ways
Mending His Vow

Hurting veterans, the women they love, and the dogs who need them come together at the Wounded Warrior Rescue.

About the Author

Kristen Iten is a night owl-ish author, and mother of three happy little owlets. She spends her working hours solving mysteries, bringing evil doers to justice, and meddling in the love lives of her imaginary friends. She suffers from an over active imagination, but doesn't really mind because it helps with the whole 'writing books thing'. She lives in a cute little town, in a cute little house, with her cute little family, and couldn't possibly be happier.

Visit www.KristenIten.com for a complete list of Kristen's books, including other books in this series!

facebook.com/kristeniten

amazon.com/author/kristeniten

bookbub.com/authors/kristen-iten

tiktok.com/@authorkristeniten